THE HUNTERS OF KANTA

THE WOLVES OF KANTA SERIES: BOOK 3

MARLENA FRANK

Edited by: Lara Zielinksy
http://lzedits.com

Cover Art by: Harvest Moon Designs
https://www.facebook.com/groups/HarvestMoonDesigns

Map by: Kelley M. Frank
http://morbidsmile.com

EB ISBN: 978-1-955854-09-2
PB ISBN: 978-1-955854-10-8
HB ISBN: 978-1-955854-11-5

To my Aunt Charmaine
For believing in me regardless of where my heart takes me.

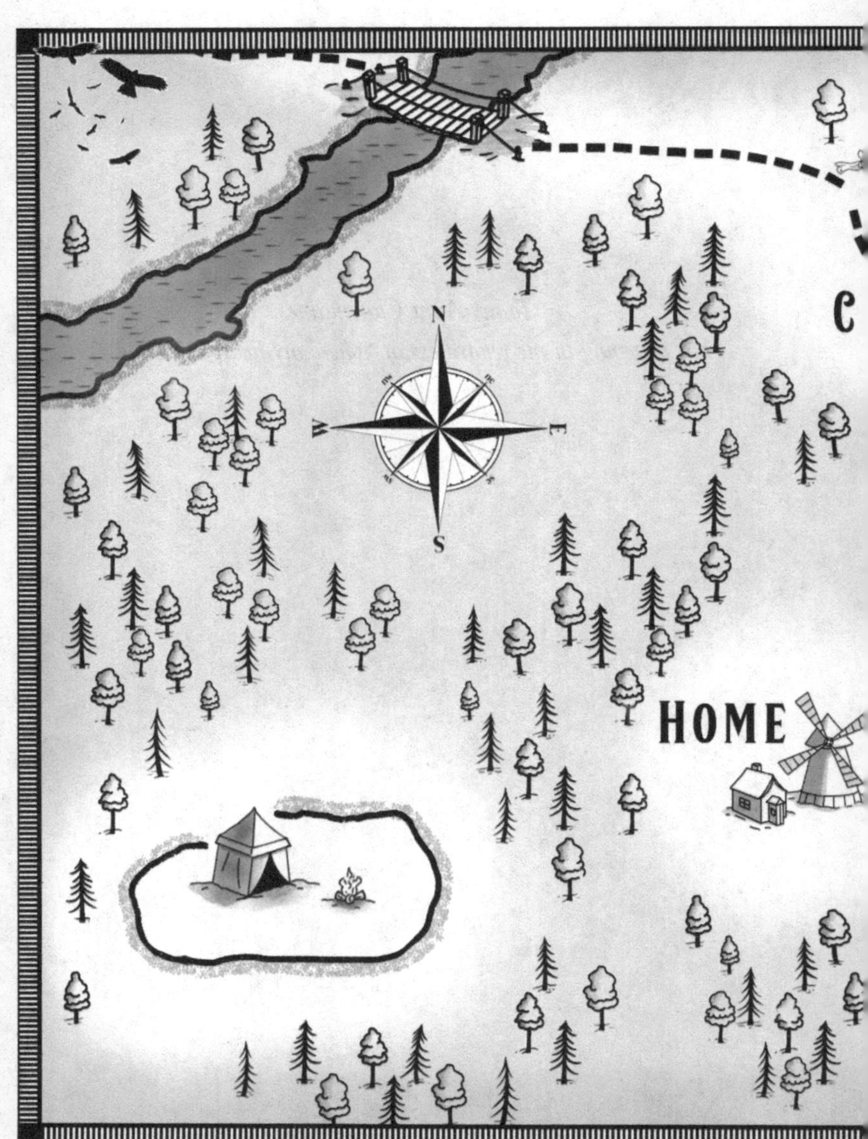

N
W
E
S
C
HOME

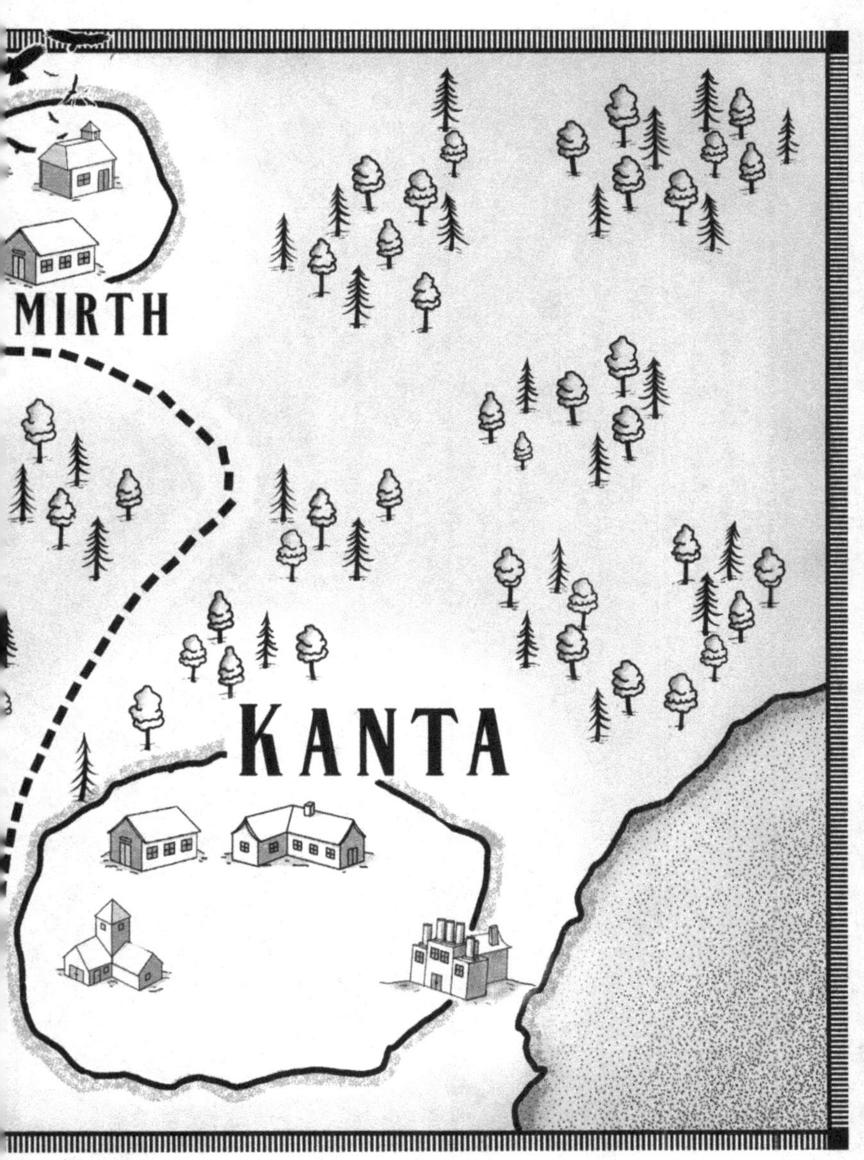

MIRTH
KANTA

PART 1

THE OUTBREAK

1

———————

FAILURES

MOONLIGHT SHONE in through the windows of the central tower of Thomas Farrell's mill. White beams of it streaked across the metal steps and down the coiling banister of the spiral staircase. In the lingering darkness, it almost looked peaceful. The mill held many secrets, many hidden places, and Mercy was one of the few permitted to know them.

At the top of the stairs, she stopped and finished lacing her bodice. Normally she would stop by the kitchen and grab some breakfast before beginning her work, but not today. She was too anxious.

She slid a hand into her pocket and felt the vial there, safe and warm. Today would be different. She would see a change. She was sure of it.

The new chemical compound she had made was a mixture of the partial cure she had created and Thomas' harmful Liquid Lead. Mercy's partial cure had worked on Andrei, allowing him to transform at will and no longer be beholden to the pull of the full moon.

Thomas' Liquid Lead was a bizarre but simple mixture strong enough to prevent a werewolf from ever changing back into a human being. It altered a werewolf's body on a cellular level. Through countless attempts, Mercy found those changes nearly impossible to revert.

Mercy's new compound was different. After completing dozens of trials, she finally had a chance to reverse the effects of the Liquid Lead. Theoretically, at least.

Her latest mixture had shown incredible promise through the dirty lens of Thomas' microscope. It had mixed well with the werewolf blood and seemed to cause some change, even with the damage to the cells from the Liquid Lead dose. She was hopeful, but knowing how resilient werewolves were, especially transformed ones, she was determined not to get too hopeful, without much luck.

Late last night, she had given one of the werewolves a dose, this time with full potency, since the other trials hadn't shown results. If it worked, if it allowed the werewolves in the laboratory to gain their human bodies again, as well as their minds… the implications could change the world. Mercy will have solved the werewolf problem plaguing the lands for over a decade.

She shook her head. She couldn't allow herself to think that far ahead or hope for the impossible. Her mind wanted to run down the path of potentials, but she couldn't let it. No, this was a time for practicality and focus. She needed to complete a successful experiment first, and then she would allow herself a small celebration. First, she needed results.

Mercy worked at the fabric along the front of her outfit, tucking pieces of the sleeveless blouse beneath the bodice to keep it from getting in the way. The leather bodice matched her trousers and boots, and, according to Leyda, would normally be unfit for a woman to wear. In Mercy's opinion, dress formality ought to have died off once werewolves had entered the lands. Long, flowy dresses and lace sleeves were fine—when you didn't have to worry about being chased down at the end of a dinner party.

In her line of work though, Mercy couldn't abide long fabrics potentially getting caught on a burner or contaminating a sample. When she first had started working, still trying to dress the way a lady ought to dress, she lost a whole week's work when her puffy linen shirt had gotten dipped in a Petri dish. She hadn't realized it for days. She had many sleepless nights afterward, wondering how much of her work she had inadvertently sabotaged.

Thomas was very understanding, having worked with chemicals often over the years. He didn't seem at all fazed by her choice of clothes. In fact, he encouraged her to wear whatever she wanted within the safety of the mill. He seemed almost relieved to have someone to share in his woes of chemical experimentation and fashion choices. Mercy had made and mended her own clothes often when she lived with her father, so she knew how to take her own measurements. Thomas sent the measurements to a tailor who lived up north. To her relief, everything fit perfectly and had made her work much easier.

Mercy laced up the front of her bodice and knotted it before taking a deep breath and testing the looseness of the fit. Mobility was another necessity, especially when working with werewolves. It didn't matter if they had their minds or not. If they were in a foul mood, Mercy would get scratched if she couldn't move fast enough. She still had scars along her forearms from her previous mistakes, one across her jawline from one particularly angry strike last year, and a nasty one along her back from when she was training under her father to be a werewolf hunter.

With her clothes now in order, Mercy went down the spiral staircase with ease. She knew where to step to keep the stairs from creaking beneath her weight. She had grown so accustomed to walking up and down the steps each day she could almost do it with her eyes closed. As she padded down the final steps, she smiled with hopeful anticipation of her results, despite her own advice against it.

At the base of the spiral staircase against the wall stood a large metal door with three great metal beams across the front, which were latched into place. Normally Thomas or Leyda had to pull each one open with their steam-powered arms, but Leyda had kindly left the laboratory door open tonight, so all Mercy had to do was pull the heavy door back a crack and slip inside.

She took a moment to check the corridor to make sure none of the werewolves were wandering. In a half-asleep daze months ago, she had come down one morning and nearly run into one of them. She shrieked, the werewolf whimpered and scampered away, and Mercy had to catch her breath for a few minutes to recover. These days, she was more careful, more aware of her surroundings. One mantra she told herself now: never expect anything to be where it should be. That included the werewolves and it made her prepared for anything. Mercy breathed in the scent of the burning lantern oil set in an alcove on the wall and focused on the shadows the flames flung against the stone corridor. Once she was certain the path was clear, she made her way down the narrow passage.

It was hard to fathom that over a year ago, she had run down to this laboratory with Thomas, escaping Carter's wild gunfire. She looked back on that time with a mixture of gratefulness to Leyda and Thomas and guilt at her own helplessness. Of course, she did not know at the time that she would ultimately spend so much time in the lab working with her own experiments, or that she would be given her own space to work. Her younger self would have balked at such responsibilities.

Mercy had learned much since then. It felt like that fear and uncertainty were a lifetime ago.

At the base of the ramp, she turned and faced the expansive room. Werewolf cages lined the walls and she gazed at the sleeping werewolves within each one. A couple of them opened their eyes blearily to look at her before nuzzling down into their fur again. Many of them she knew, but several more had arrived since she had begun working the lab. Each had their own history, personalities, and annoyances. One large wolf with jet black fur let out a sharp-toothed yawn before glancing at her with bleary yellow eyes before curling up again and going back to sleep. In their defense, it was very early for Mercy dropping by and they were used to sleeping in.

The closest cage sat empty and had been for months. It used to belong to Andrei, and he wanted it kept for him "just in case." At the time, Mercy was a little offended that he didn't trust her chemical compound to fend off the nightly transformations, but then again, she couldn't truly be mad at him. She had seen firsthand the painful and terrifying transformations. Andrei no longer needed the cage since he could control his transformations now. In fact, he had his own room and bed and frequently slept in late. She regularly teased him about that, but she didn't mind really. After all he had been through, he deserved a little comfort.

"Sorry to wake everyone," Mercy whispered to the slumbering werewolves as she crossed the room. "Go back to sleep. It's okay." She headed for a cage she knew well, one that contained not one werewolf, but two.

At first it looked like the cage had a giant ball of fur, but slowly Mercy made out the gray muzzle of the little girl poking out of the sea of dark silver fur around her. The child had her mouth wide open, tongue lolled to the side, and was snoring loudly. Mercy grinned and wondered if she slept the same way.

"Ruth? Good morning," Mercy said in a hushed voice as she crouched down beside the cage.

One amber eye opened, tired and annoyed.

Mercy gave an apologetic smile and sat down with her legs criss-crossed. She gave a little wave.

The child yawned and turned over, curling up against her mother's warm belly.

"I'm sorry to wake you," she whispered, "but I was hoping the dose I gave you last night helped. Was there… anything?"

The annoyance in Ruth's gaze told her the answer already, but she had to hope. There was simply no way the chemical was completely ineffective. The sample under the microscope couldn't lie. She had seen something happen with her own eyes. Maybe Ruth only remained in her werewolf form for her daughter's comfort. Maybe she just looked annoyed, but she wasn't really—she was a werewolf after all.

Ruth stared steadily and shook her head.

"Seriously? Nothing?" Mercy asked again.

Snorting in annoyance, Ruth shook her head again, more vigorously this time, and she gave a low growl as well. All the hope and excitement Mercy had built up about the experiment deflated in an instant.

"Not even a pinkie? No loss of fur? You didn't even feel a little sick? Like a stomach ache?"

Ruth rolled her eyes and grumbled.

"Come on now, there has to be something that came of the last dose. You said you felt weird at first, so there had to be something with it, right?" Mercy gripped the bars.

Ruth's frustration turned to resignation. She lowered her gaze and shook her head again with a whimper. Clearly she was as disappointed as Mercy. Of course she would be. It was another broken promise, another chance at being human dashed away.

Mercy took a deep breath and reached a hand through the bars, unable to go any farther than her elbow. She laid a hand on Ruth's shoulder, feeling the prickliness of her coarse coat. "I'm sorry to keep getting your hopes up. I appreciate you volunteering. I guess I get nervous and impatient. There has to be a cure for you all, I know it. And I will find it somehow, okay?"

Glancing down at her daughter, Ruth sighed. Mercy didn't know the girl's name or how old she was. All she knew was Ruth was fiercely protective of her and the girl hardly ever left her side. How long had it been since Ruth saw the girl in her human form? Had the child been a werewolf longer than she had been human? That last question made her heart hurt.

"I'll find a way, I promise."

Ruth met her gaze again and nodded. Mercy saw the despair and hopelessness under the surface, sadness Ruth couldn't conceal despite having the body of a hairy beast.

Mercy rubbed Ruth's shoulder, hoping to give some reassurance no matter how small. Climbing back to her feet, she sighed. The experiment had failed. Okay. She determined to keep trying until she found something, anything, to help. The Liquid Lead was too crudely made to be so permanent. At least, she hoped so.

She went to her office attached to the laboratory. It used to be Thomas' office, but after she created a partial cure with Andrei's help, he let her have the whole space. She stepped inside and lit a few candles to give the room some light. The smell of oil filled the room before Mercy closed the door. Then she pressed her forehead against the wood and gave a deep sigh.

"Damn," she whispered to herself. "Damn, damn, damn."

She had failed. Again.

It wasn't even a diluted compound that time, it had been at its full potency. Still, it hadn't even fazed Ruth. She hadn't mention any pains or bad reactions, which was a mercy. But it was as if Mercy had used a placebo. Whatever the Liquid Lead did to werewolf bodies, it seemed to freeze them in place so they couldn't move forward or backward in the transformation process. Hormones had to have something to do with it since there were such wildly different reactions between men and women, and whether it reverted the mind, but she had no idea what that meant. Maybe if Mercy had received a proper education instead of the cobbled together version from her father… No, she shouldn't think like that. She was lucky to have had the limited education she had, not to mention the ability to do this work at all.

Liquid Lead wasn't all powerful. Leyda was a living example of that. Thomas had given her additional treatments, poorly researched options according to his notes, but they had made noticeable differences. However, Leyda was now full of such a hodgepodge of chemicals Mercy wasn't sure if any cure she made would work on her. It was upsetting, and whatever connection she once had with Leyda, no matter how tenuous, was slowly breaking because of her jealousy of Andrei's partial cure.

Leyda wasn't a human being, and she wasn't a werewolf anymore. She was stuck somewhere in between. She considered herself a monster, but really she proved that there was a chance. Mercy had to trust her own intuition and not get bogged down by the inevitable failures. Those same failures had made Thomas turn away from trying at all, and she couldn't let it do the same to her. If that happened, there truly would be no hope. Nobody else was going to step in to save the werewolves. Only she had that power.

Mercy turned around to look at her office, leaning her back against the door to take in the room.

After the success of the partial vaccine she had created with Andrei's help, Mercy had been given the entire room by Thomas, who left behind any supplies or books she had said she wanted. She had never owned so many things in her entire life. It was daunting, but she had taken it upon herself to make sense of the disorganized mess Thomas had left behind.

Half the room was dedicated to research and reading, with journals filled with notes, organized by topic, alongside scientific texts from anatomy to chemistry to the few on werewolf study. Those she had pored over so many times the pages were falling out of the binding.

The other half of the room was her laboratory space. Beakers, vials, and burners lined the table, with distilleries in the corner where she made batches of the partial vaccines. In all honesty, she was sometimes so busy with making the vaccine that she had little time to do research and experimentation. Perhaps that was why she had put so much weight on the few times she could squeeze in an experiment, a few trials, or a new compound. It was always a struggle.

Enthusiasm and praise had given her unrealistic expectations that the next compound would be as easy to discover as the first, but her many failures said otherwise. She wanted to go to her lab table, to start in on her next attempt at a viable compound, but she restrained herself. As much as she wanted to try something new, she had other tasks that demanded her attention, especially today.

Today was a special day, one that she had anticipated and feared for months. She would travel with Andrei and Leyda to visit the local werewolf camp of Kanta. They would demonstrate the partial cure Andrei had taken and hopefully, with their trust, administer it to others. She was to meet Thomas in the reception room half an hour before dawn, the best time to go out while still avoiding most of the townspeople of Kanta. That gave her two hours to work.

Mercy pushed herself off the door and went to the distilleries. They would need plenty of stock to bring with them because they did not know how many werewolves would be there. It had been a year since her last visit, since Henry's death, and since she had met Andrei.

Her hands shook as she picked up a basket of needles that she had made the evening before and began preparing them. She was meticulous with every measurement, wary of making any mistake when so much was on the line.

She couldn't afford another failure.

WITH A BASKET of injection needles in each hand, a biscuit in her mouth, and her pockets full of spare cloth for the disguise she would need, Mercy stepped out of the tower. Her failed experiment with Ruth had delayed her longer than expected, mostly because she had trouble motivating herself. Crafting a fresh batch of the partial vaccine had taken a long time. She had filled fifty needles, capping each one off with cork to keep herself from getting stabbed. Though it was still dark, dawn was close. A bright, full moon lit up the sky, but in the distance she could hear birds singing. Autumn was quickly approaching, accentuated by a cold breeze across the catwalk.

Mercy bit down harder on her biscuit to keep from losing it and started her trek through each of the grinder rooms. Gone were the werewolves in chains at the base of the chambers. They had been replaced with steam-powered technology created by Thomas. In her opinion, the grinders had never run so smoothly or so quietly. It was an enormous change from the cruelty imposed on the werewolves when she first had arrived at Farrell Mill. It had taken convincing, but she was proud of Thomas for making the right choice.

Moving quickly through grinder chambers three, two, and finally one, Mercy reached the reception room. She was probably a little late, but Thomas would have to deal with it. He could have come down to help her if he really wanted her on time. She pulled the heavy door to the reception room back with a few fingers, wiggled her foot into the gap, and used her leg to pull it open. She almost tipped one basket in the process.

As the door slammed shut behind her, Mercy stepped inside. She came to a complete stop, staring.

Cages sat all around her. Every one of them contained a snarling, biting, enraged werewolf. Mercy's body went rigid.

She had gotten so used to working with the calm werewolves down in the lab that it was easy to forget how dangerous they were at peak ferocity. Her heart raced in her chest, her hands got sweaty, and a pit formed in her gut. At least twenty of them surrounded her, all furious and clearly hungry. She reminded herself they were caged, to refrain from running out of the room and back to the tower.

Amber eyes turned to her, as though smelling her fear. One werewolf gave an ear-piercing howl that made her instinctively shrink inward as a shiver sped down her spine. She backed away toward the door, seriously considering leaving and returning to the silence and safety of the laboratory. Any place looked better than this.

"Ah, Mercy. Perfect!"

Thomas Farrell stepped out from behind several cages. He adjusted his fur trimmed, crimson short cape over his shoulder, and reached for one of the baskets she still gripped tightly in her hands. It took a moment of him pulling on the basket before she finally realized and let it go.

He glanced around the room, his expression sheepish. "I'm sorry for the surprise. We had an unexpected delivery arrive this morning and we're running low on your inoculations." He gestured to the basket. "These came at the perfect time."

Mercy used her free hand to remove the biscuit from her mouth so she could talk. "Where did they all come from?" She nibbled at the bread as he spoke, trying to stop herself from shaking. She couldn't bolt. As terrifying as this room was, and as much as her instincts told her to flee, she had to fight it. This was her work now.

"Hunters brought them by last night and this morning. They had to make multiple trips. None of them have been dosed with Liquid Lead thankfully." Thomas stifled a yawn. "Apparently there's been an outbreak in Crowsmirth, about half a day's ride north of us. I had to close our doors to sales this morning, not just because of the trip you all are making, but because I don't have room for any more." He put the basket on his desk and shook his head. "I hate having to do that. The ones we don't take—they'll be killed."

Mercy winced. "I know," she said and then finished her biscuit. "I wish we could tell them to wait, but that would make us look suspicious. Are those lords up north still paying for each head?"

He gave a grim nod. "Unfortunately. What's worse is that they're upping their payments because of the outbreak. I can only pay so much for them live and not drugged like this, especially now that it's a loss for my business."

He put his hands up at Mercy's narrowed gaze.

"Not that I mind having a loss. This is good work we're doing and is far more… humane, as you stated before. I'm simply not made of money. Those lords, on the other hand, are rolling in it."

Mercy frowned, taking in the room again with renewed interest. There were enough werewolves here to fill over one grinder. That's assuming the public still thought that's what Thomas was buying them for: manual labor. People were clever. They would start talking, wondering what was happening to the many werewolves brought here—especially if they saw the room this full. As beneficial as this work was, it could be short-lived if they weren't careful. They didn't want hunters prying into the workings of Farrell Mill.

"We'll have to keep the mill closed for new purchases for a while, maybe a week or two," Mercy said.

Thomas pursed his lips. "If we do that, more will be slaughtered."

"Not if we take out the source."

He crossed his arms, clearly not convinced.

She continued. "If they had an outbreak in Crowsmirth, then there has to be at least one camp those werewolves are coming from in the woods. If we can get to them before the hunters do, we can give them the partial cure, and take away the hunters' source of income."

Thomas looked around the room, his brows furrowed. "That's going to leave some angry hunters."

"Better than dead werewolves," she countered.

Thomas licked his lips and gave a short nod. "That's a good point. But do you think it's wise to go after two camps back to back? Assuming there's only one in Crowsmirth?"

Mercy pulled out her strips of cloth from one of her many pockets and started wrapping them around her face. "Do we have a choice? If the outbreak is this bad, how many people are going to be killed, do you think?"

He frowned and pinched the bridge of his nose. "Dozens, possibly hundreds, if the outbreak is large enough. We can't have that."

Before Mercy could respond, the door to the catwalk opened and Leyda and Andrei entered the room. If the caged werewolves had gotten loud at Mercy's entrance, then they were furious when those two appeared. Leyda, always prepared, had already put on her facial disguise. She did it perfectly every time, somehow masking her very obvious muzzle and leaving only her eyes exposed. Andrei's hair was askew and his eyes were wide as he stared at the caged werewolves. This was way earlier than he was used to getting out of bed, and stepping into a room full of incensed, snarling werewolves probably wasn't the best wake-up call.

Mercy went over and took his hand. He gave her a bewildered smile as he continued eyeing the room. In his opposite hand, he held his own bundle of cloth wrappings. They would need to put their disguises on before leaving.

Leyda gestured them to the front of the room. So much for small talk. Leyda didn't look back as she headed to the front door. She was probably excited to see Rose again, but Mercy would have appreciated a greeting, or at least allowing them time to get ready.

Mercy put her basket on the floor and pulled out her wrappings. She and Andrei got to work disguising themselves for the outdoors.

If anyone saw Mercy was a young woman, she could be targeted by hunters and captured by traffickers. She had bound her chest downstairs in the laboratory before coming up, and traded her sleeveless blouse and bodice for a loose-fitting tunic instead. The tunic did more than hide her curves, it also hid her pistol with silver bullets. Andrei wore a facial disguise to keep his identity hidden. He had worked as an apprentice at the apothecary before he was turned, and if they saw him, he might be captured or killed for being a werewolf.

Unfortunately they weren't as good at donning their disguises as Leyda, and it took them several minutes to get fully covered. Thomas came over with a few rags and used them to cover up the contents of the basket at their feet.

"There you go," he said as he stood back up. "Can't have anyone seeing those. They'll raise far too many questions."

"Thank you," Andrei said, tying his wrappings behind his head. "Sorry I was late. I didn't know we were leaving so early."

Thomas clapped his shoulder with a wide smile, "Neither did I. But if you hurry, you might catch up with her still."

Mercy nodded and grabbed the basket. Leyda was the only one who knew the way to the camp. Without her, they would easily get lost. So, in true Leyda fashion, she was trying to lose them.

Together they rushed past the remaining cages as the werewolves howled and snarled in the excitement. Mercy glanced back at Thomas, wondering if he could handle all the werewolves on his own. He stood at the back of the room with a smile and his arms crossed, the basket of needles on his desk behind him.

He would have his work cut out for him, but then again, so did they.

———

THE SUN HADN'T QUITE BROKEN over the horizon, but it was close. A cold breeze swept across the dirt roads, tossing dust and debris into the air. The streets of Kanta were oddly busy for so early in the morning.

Mercy noticed far more hunters were out than usual. She recognized them by their firearms, their vehicles, and their padded outfits meant to disguise them in the forest. Despite the excess foot traffic and additional vehicles she didn't recognize, people got out of the way for her and Andrei.

Rumors circled around Kanta about the strange, bandaged people that Thomas Farrell hired to work at his mill. Some people thought they were murderers, others thought they had leprosy, but no one knew the truth. That suited Mercy just fine. She preferred them to be afraid of them. That meant they wouldn't try to approach or ask silly questions, and hopefully it would make them think twice before attacking them.

Without her bandages, Leyda looked like a partially

transformed werewolf and would be killed on the spot if she were discovered. Mercy knew human traffickers who posed as werewolf hunters in the city would love to get their hands on her. Being a woman was dangerous in the vile city of Kanta. If anyone found out that Andrei was a werewolf, or even a partially cured werewolf, he could be beheaded or shot.

"A werewolf is a werewolf." Mercy could practically hear the excuse the hunters would use when they sent his head to the lords up north to get some measly payment. It was the same sort of phrase her father had once told her.

Whenever any of the bandaged people who worked at Farrell Mill walked down the street together, people noticed. They kept their distance, but gawked and gossiped behind closed doors.

Mercy glanced at the jailhouse as they passed by. The building had no windows but had only a single, open door at the front. The smell of sweat and urine drifted out as they passed by. Who had they made the new deputy to replace Pillsby? She still remembered the last time she saw his body: Pillsby laying dead in an alley, being eaten by Henry, a fully transformed werewolf. Her stomach dropped as the memory of that night struck again: the brimstone scent of Henry's blood on the dirt, the cold breeze against her face, and the hot tears streaming down her cheeks.

Add that to the long list of traumatic experiences that would haunt her for the rest of her life.

Mercy shook herself as Leyda came into view. She stood at the edge of town, waiting for them. Pushing the memories and the pain away from her mind, Mercy focused on the task at hand. She had to keep her head straight. This was no time to show weakness, especially with so many eyes on them. She clutched the basket closer beneath her elbow and headed to meet up with Leyda. With Andrei on one side of her and Leyda on the other, Mercy felt stronger.

The work they were doing was important. It not only would protect the people of Kanta, but it would also protect the werewolves who were victims as well.

She didn't have time to waste on the past. Right now, they had werewolves to save.

2

______

DUST

SUNLIGHT GLITTERED DOWN through the pines and scattered on the underbrush as they made their way through the forest and toward the werewolf camp. Leyda led the way, followed by Andrei, and Mercy struggled to keep up with them. Leyda kept a fast pace, almost into a light jog, once they delved into the trees. At first, Mercy didn't complain. She assumed Leyda was simply putting distance between them and Kanta, but after a mile or so at that pace, she had to say something.

"Leyda!" she called out, already breathing hard, even though they were only a fraction into the journey.

Leyda paused and turned toward her, crossing her arms.

"Can we slow up, please? I'm not like you two. I can't keep up this pace." Mercy came to a stop before her, putting a hand on a tree as she panted. The bark of the pine tree was sharp and brittle under her fingertips.

"Yeah, what's the rush?" Andrei asked her. "I don't

think the camp is going to disappear if we take our time. We have all day."

He wasn't even winded. Sometimes it was difficult being the only human in a group full of werewolves. Mercy had a hard time asking for help on a normal day, but it was far worse when she was physically the weakest of all of them. It didn't help that Leyda regularly exploited that weakness.

This friction between her and Leyda had formed when Mercy developed her partial cure. At first, she thought Leyda was jealous of her abilities, but as time went by, she suspected Leyda was jealous of Andrei. Mercy couldn't help the fact that Leyda's condition resulted from layers of poorly understood chemical attempts. Undoing that work was a feat Thomas couldn't even crack.

Whatever the reason, the friction had only grown worse. It had started with Leyda questioning her late night research on Andrei to attacking Mercy when the untested treatment actually worked to revert Andrei's lycanthropy. Now she was being childish, intentionally out-pacing her on an inoculation expedition. She was probably around ten years Mercy's senior, but it was hard to tell sometimes from her actions.

Leyda glanced to the path ahead and then back to Mercy. Her dark eyes looked her up and down, assessing her, judging her. Mercy's anger boiled up.

Then bubbled over. "You wish I hadn't come, is that it?" she snapped.

Andrei's eyes widened as he looked between the two of them.

"You slow us down," Leyda stated simply. "I asked Thomas if we could leave you behind, and he refused. He said your presence would be useful, not that I fully understand what he meant by that."

Mercy couldn't believe what she was hearing. Pushing off the tree, she stood up straighter. She'd had a growth spurt in the last few months, making her slightly taller than Leyda, a fact that always seemed to irk her. Mercy reveled in it.

"Do you even remember what happened last time we came?" Mercy asked, advancing on her. "If I hadn't been here, the pack would have either shot you or run you out with torches in hand."

Leyda grunted in annoyance. "And if you hadn't been there to slow us down, I could have gotten Andrei back to the mill in plenty of time before sundown. A human should not be tagging along on these tasks. It's too dangerous, and you risk compromising our mission."

"Compromising our mission!" Mercy balled her fists. "Did you forget I made this?" She held the basket up for Leyda to see.

Leyda rolled her eyes. "How could I possibly forget? Everyone keeps praising you about it. Hell, Thomas redesigned his whole mill based on your request. He won't stop talking about your supposed brilliance. It makes me sick!"

"Um, ladies?" Andrei stepped between them and gently pushed them apart. "I know you two really want to fight and all, but can we do this later? We're running out of daylight and I'm pretty sure that's a hunter trap over there."

Mercy blinked and swallowed down the retort she had prepared. She turned to see a structure in the distance, heavily disguised by thick tree limbs and underbrush. It was a werewolf cage.

Her feet starting moving before she realized it, her curiosity burning for an answer to the question she feared to ask.

"Mercy!" Andrei hissed, but she ignored him. Leyda whispered something under her breath. Thankfully Mercy couldn't make out the words.

She stepped over a rotted out log, pulled aside some briars that looked painfully familiar, and finally she reached the cage itself. If there had been anything attached to it, there was no sign of it now. She crouched down at the base and heard a squirrel rush off into the foliage.

With her bare hands, she pulled away the leaves, dirt, and pine straw built up beside it until, finally, she could see the base of the cage itself. A piece of wood went along the edge from one side of the cage to the other. She recognized it.

It was a modified cage, meant to be easily removed from the back of a truck with a few simple movements. It was the cage her father had built. She had helped him build it. She remembered holding the cold metal screws in her tiny hands as her father attached them to the bottom. The wooden rail even had his uneven cut that he refused to admit was crooked.

She turned and leaned her back against the cage. Her eyes were hot and the scent of flowers on the breeze did little to quell her pain. In the distance, she saw the road she and her father had taken that day. The road that led back toward her home.

A warm hand reached for hers and she gripped it, recognizing the feel of Andrei instantly.

"Leyda is waiting," he said nervously, and then went quiet when he met her gaze. He rubbed her shoulder. "Are you okay? What's wrong?"

"This cage." Her throat didn't want to cooperate, and she had to swallow to get the words out. "This was my father's cage for trapping werewolves. I helped him build it. We modified it together when I was little."

Andrei turned back toward it, taking it in with renewed interest. She gestured to the crooked wood at the bottom and the rusty screws. He rubbed her back. "Take a moment, okay? Take a deep breath in."

Mercy did as he asked, taking a deep breath in and slowly letting it out again. Roses, that's what she smelled. There had to be some in bloom nearby. She let the perfumed air out slowly and felt a little calmer, but that did nothing to take the lump from forming in her throat.

"Wait, so if this is his cage… does that mean you were attacked near here?"

She nodded and took another deep breath of the roses. Tears came to her eyes. An image came to her suddenly of her father laying out on the ground, the bullet hole bloody and bright against the brown leaves and pine straw as blood pooled around his head. A bunch of roses swayed over him in the breeze. She shook herself as tears fell, wetting the bandages wrapped around her face.

Andrei took the basket she still held and put an arm

around her shoulders. He turned her away from Leyda in the distance. "Hey, it's okay."

He folded her against his chest and she cried against him, unable to keep the pain away any longer, unable to keep the emotions from overflowing.

"Shh, I know." He held her for a long time and let her cry. "I'm so sorry, Mercy."

It seemed like no matter what she did or who she became, she could never escape her past or forget that terrible day. Every time she thought she had overcome it, the loss overwhelmed her all over again. She had only that morning thought of that pain as being a lifetime ago, but life had a strange way of reminding her she wasn't so different from that terrified girl in the woods. She was the same person no matter how much time passed, and the pain was just as fresh, even knowing all she did now.

Finally she pulled back and looked up into his gorgeous brown eyes. "Thank you for understanding," she whispered.

He wiped the tears from her eyes as best he could around the bandages. She couldn't help but smile at his attempts.

"I know what it's like to lose your family. I was the only survivor in my household after the pack of werewolves found us in the night." He shook his head, his gaze distant. "I thought about doing terrible things when it happened. Things I would never dream of doing now."

Mercy sniffled and cleared her throat. "Like what?"

He shook his head, a sad expression passing over his

gaze. How much she wished she could see his full face to understand him better.

"Doesn't matter. All that matters is that I didn't do it. If I had, I never would have met you and that would be the biggest tragedy of all."

He gave her a squeeze, and she wrapped her arms around him, hugging him tight. "That means I would have never met you either. That would have definitely been a tragedy."

Andrei pulled away and handed her back the basket.

She gave a wry smile. "I don't think I'm all that great. There has to be something better than me to be thankful for." She gave a weak laugh.

"Not in my book," he put an arm around her shoulders. "Come on, Leyda's going to burst a blood vessel if we take much longer down here."

Mercy wanted to laugh, but she knew he was right.

When they climbed the overgrown hill, Leyda stood there with her arms crossed, glaring daggers at them both.

"If you two are done making out around old werewolf cages, we have some living werewolves to go aid," she snapped. "Disgusting," she muttered and headed down the path before they had even finished climbing back up the hill.

Andrei snickered at her comment and Mercy smiled. Leyda complained, but she could have left them if she wanted. Instead, she had waited, so that had to mean something.

Mercy looked back over her shoulder once more, knowing eventually the underbrush would consume the cage completely. A cold wind came again, bringing the smell of roses. Mercy turned away from it.

Good, she thought. Let the land reclaim any memory of that day. Let the natural world take it back to the earth. She wanted no more reminders of what she had lost, of the life she had once lived, or the painful guilt of her father's death.

Let the world move on. Let the past turn to dust.

Mercy couldn't change the past, but she could shape the future.

HER HEART HURT from finding that damn cage and her eyes still ached from crying, but walking helped. Focusing on their mission helped. As the trees thinned out and more sunlight poured through, Mercy was grateful. They had been walking for hours and after the short run earlier, her feet were tired.

In the distance, she spotted the clearing and knew they were close. She glanced to Andrei, expecting to see him just as excited as she felt, but he looked upset, maybe even solemn.

Mercy slipped her hand into his and he blinked as if he had forgotten she was even there.

"Aren't you looking forward to being with your pack mates again?" She asked, hoping to see his eyes light up with a smile.

Instead he glanced away from her, a haunted look in his eyes. "I wish I could say yes, but I didn't exactly leave on the best of terms last time. And it's going to be weird not seeing Henry at his post."

Her stomach dropped at his words. Henry. She had forgotten about him. It had been so long since that night. So much had happened. Still, how could she forget him? She had been the one to shoot him and had watched him transform back into his human form.

Not knowing what to say or do, she squeezed Andrei's hand and hoped that could convey what she couldn't put into words. He returned it. That was hardly enough to make up for losing his friend, but she knew nothing she did or said would ever make up for her actions.

As if reading her mind, Andrei stated, "It was in self defense, I know that. Henry knew the risk when he came after us, but it still hurts, you know? He was one of my only friends, like a father to me here." He paused for a moment before adding, "I know you didn't know him very well, but he was a good person."

"I know," she said. "If he was your friend, he had to be. And he deserved better than that."

Andrei started to say more, but Leyda held a hand up. They both went silent, scanning the open clearing and looking for any sign of trouble.

The last time Mercy came here, she and Leyda had been shot at. This time, she had no idea what to expect. Would the pack see them as friendly or as hostile? For all they knew the pack could have entirely new members and nobody would know them, let alone let them enter the camp. These were unknown variables she probably should have thought about before coming here.

Leyda held her hands up as she approached. "We mean you no harm. We are merely here to help you."

A boy who couldn't have been older than ten or eleven stood up from behind a large tree stump. He had dirty blonde hair, pale sunburned skin, and clothes that was falling apart from the number of holes and claw marks on it. In his hands he held a shotgun that was almost as big as he was.

"Stop right there or I'll shoot!"

"Damn," Andrei whispered, his eyes wide in shock.

Mercy agreed with him. That kid was way too young to be out defending the boundary of the werewolf camp. She remembered what Andrei had told her the last time she had come with Leyda. The youngest were chosen for this work, but even Andrei had an older adult like Henry around to guide him and make sure he didn't shoot at someone he shouldn't—or himself. This kid was out here on his own.

If this was who the camp chose to keep them protected, what did that mean for the camp itself? Mercy hadn't considered the shape the pack members were in before, but now she did, and she was worried. Most of them were very sick. One of the older ones had a terrible cough too. She remembered the way the others looked at her when she hacked badly, as though expecting her to keel over at any minute. What had happened in the last year?

"It's okay," Leyda said. Her voice was calm even though Mercy saw her hands shaking. "We're not here to hurt anyone. We're here to help."

Andrei stepped forward and placed a hand to his

chest. "I'm from this camp, and so is Leyda." He gestured to Leyda, and she nodded. "She's right, we're here to help. You can put the gun down."

The boy looked between them, confusion and suspicion flitting across his face.

"Leyda? I don't know that name. Sounds made up."

Andrei exchanged a worried look with Leyda. "What about Andrei? Or Henry?" Andrei was trying to sound casual, but Mercy could see the nerves in his posture. He was ready to drop to the ground in an instant if needed.

Finally the boy put the gun down. "Andrei and Henry, they were the guards a long time ago. The elders said they ran away from their posts."

Andrei shifted uncomfortably. "Yeah, well, I'm back now. Can you let us in so we can talk to everybody?"

The boy strapped the gun onto his back with practiced ease and hopped down from an old crate he was using as a step ladder. Once on the ground, Mercy noted he was even shorter than she first thought. Maybe the boy was more like eight or nine.

He waved them over.

"What's your name, kid?" Andrei asked.

"Finn."

Andrei grinned. "It's good to meet you, Finn."

The boy turned, ignoring Andrei's greeting, and waved them to follow. "It's this way. Try to keep up."

Andrei shook his head and sighed. Mercy took his hand again.

"What does he mean that happened a long time

ago?" Andrei asked in a hoarse whisper. "That was just last year, right?"

Mercy nodded. "A year is a long time to a kid. Are you really more insulted by that than by him implying you ran away from your post?"

He pulled her closer so he could link his arm with hers. "Honestly? Yeah! I just assumed he was being a snotty kid."

Finn turned around suddenly. "You know I can hear you, right? You were a pretty snotty guard if you ask me! Abandoning everybody and running off with that human girl."

Mercy had to hold back a snicker.

Andrei groaned. "Really?"

"Easy," Mercy said. "Let him be. We're here to do a job, remember?"

Andrei rubbed at the back of his head. "Yeah, well, if we're one short, I know who we can leave off the list."

3

———

RISKS

THIS WAS NOT the werewolf camp Mercy remembered. She would have never thought that conditions could get any worse, but they had.

Pools of blood were everywhere, covering the muddy ground all around the camp. Each one drew a cacophony of vermin, from flies to mosquitos to even a few rats. Mercy remembered seeing them last time she had come to the camp and had discovered that it was from the werewolves' nightly transformations. At the time, they tried to transform at the farthest edges of the camp to keep from contaminating where they lived, but clearly that wasn't being practiced any longer. Sickness hung in the air like a dew, covering everything and everyone. The great bonfire that used to be the center of the camp had been reduced to a few flickering flames. What had once been a population of twenty to thirty, had reduced to, maybe, ten.

The ramshackle lean-tos that had bordered the clearing were gone. Now the only evidence that anyone lived here were mold-smelling blankets spread out on the ground and the smell of urine and feces not far off.

A blonde woman with a pale, sunburned face who must have been in her thirties lay beside the dwindling fire. Her hair was a tangle of dirt and branches. She stared up at the clear sky, but she didn't seem to see it. Her mouth moved, but no words came out. Mercy wasn't sure if she was hallucinating or praying. Either way it was disturbing.

Finn put a log on the fire and stoked the flames with a long branch as though it might keep the camp alive. He didn't look at the squalor or the pain. Instead, he kept his eyes on his work, as though this was all he did day in and day out. He clenched his jaw. Mercy shook her head. It was so sad to see someone so young taking on so much and believing he could truly keep them all alive. It was an impossible feat.

"Is she okay?" Andrei asked, gesturing to the blonde woman.

Mercy and Finn glanced to her and Finn blinked. He gasped, dropped the stick and his shotgun, and rushed to her side. He leaned his head close to hers so that his ear was merely inches away from her lips. Maybe she had been trying to say something. Mercy shivered.

"Water. You want some water, Emily? Is that right?" Finn asked.

She gave the briefest of nods.

The boy nodded, ran over to a metal bucket that had seen better days, scooped out some water with a crude, wooden brown, and brought it back to her.

Mercy watched as he held her head up so she wouldn't choke as he poured the water into her mouth.

Mercy placed a hand to her own mouth, trying to stay present in what she was seeing. That woman could have been dying, yet Mercy merely had thought she was praying to herself. She rubbed her index finger against the wrappings on her lips, feeling the texture of the old fabric.

The disease did this. It ravaged the people who called this camp their home. It broke their spirits first, and if the hunters didn't kill them in the night, then it broke down their bodies. Night after night it ravaged their immune system, their sleep schedule, and their ability to recover from the constant onslaught. She saw it wear down Andrei before she gave him the partial vaccine. The disease tore at their bodies until it killed them.

Andrei. She glanced over to him. He wasn't shocked like Mercy was. He stared with stern eyes and his hands balled into fists. He was angry. If he hadn't chosen to come back with her that day, this would have been his fate. It would have destroyed him.

She understood now why Finn was so young, so inexperienced, and so quick to anger. Watching him care for Emily, she saw a lot of Andrei's frustration in him. He was the only one capable of doing anything at the camp, so he had to do everything. He was far too young to carry such a burden, but the disease didn't care. Eventually when the adults were all dead, it would take him too. Mercy winced at the thought.

Finn lay Emily back down on the ground before

running back to scoop up more water. Andrei kneeled down to hold Emily up so Finn didn't have to struggle so much. His balled fists loosened and became gentle as Finn tipped more water into Emily's mouth. Andrei had probably done this before, she realized with a shudder. He had held his friends as they died. No wonder he went to join Mercy. This was not a life, this was a slow inevitable death.

Leyda wrapped her arms around herself as she walked around the camp, studying faces. She glanced to Emily and at the two boys giving her water, set her jaw, and walked a little faster. She looked scared.

Mercy approached Finn as he dripped more water down Emily's throat. "How long has she been like this?"

"At least a week. I can't get her to eat anymore, but she must be eating something at night when she's transformed, I just don't know what it is." He glanced to Mercy with suspicion clouding his words. "Who are you people, anyway?"

Mercy considered this. It wasn't the first time she had questioned what names or aliases they should call themselves. Part of her wanted to give her real name, but she remembered the suspicion Henry and Andrei had the last time she and Leyda had come to the camp. Henry had been so worried he almost hadn't let her inside.

Leyda and Andrei might be comfortable giving their names, and that might be okay for this camp, but it would be dangerous for other locations. It was better if an alias gained renown rather than real names.

She thought of the people of Kanta who parted

when Thomas Farrell's hired hunters walked past. She thought of the suspicious looks out the windows and the respect they had within the city. Then she thought of the words she had written on her werewolf hunting license at the sheriff's office a lifetime ago.

"We are the Wolves of Kanta."

He glanced up at her quickly, his jaw tensed as though trying to decide if he should bolt.

"We're here to help you all live again," Mercy said, making her tone as kindly as she could.

He studied her for a moment before shaking his head. "Sounds like a scam, not gonna lie."

"It's not," Andrei said, frowning as he held Emily in his arms. The poor woman was barely conscious and her eyes were glassy. "I'm living proof. And once Emily feels better, I'll show you." He gave Finn a reassuring glance, but Mercy could see the pain in his eyes.

"Where is Rose?" Leyda called. She had ventured to the far end of the camp to look at someone asleep under a pile of dirty blankets. "Where is she? I can't find her." She paced back and forth on the opposite side of the bonfire, balling her hands into fists even as her voice broke. "I've looked everywhere."

Finn shook his head and his dirty blond hair fell into his eyes. "She didn't come back to camp."

"What do you mean?" Leyda stalked over, her eyes glassy though the rest of her body looked tense enough to snap.

Finn looked between Mercy and Andrei before climbing to his feet. "One day she wasn't here any longer. We all usually come back each morning, gather here at camp, and lick our wounds. One morning she didn't return."

Leyda took a step toward him, her eyes glinting in the fire light. She looked ready to pounce. She spoke in a small, fragile voice that didn't match her posture. "How long ago?"

Finn raked a hand through his hair. Mercy spotted blood in his dirty blond hair, still there from the transformation the night before. "Three months ago, I think? It's hard to tell time sometimes out here. I used to keep track better than I do now." He glanced down to Emily, his face contorting with worry.

Leyda's limbs went limp, and she crouched slowly to the ground before sitting down completely. She put her hand to her mouth, heedless of the careful wrappings around her face. "I told her I would return for her. I told her to wait for me. She promised me she would stay safe. *She promised me.*" Her hands shook as she stared into the fire, tears streaming down her cheeks. She dropped her head into her hands and let out a great wail.

The sound was unlike any Mercy had heard from her, and the intensity of it tore through her body, ripped into her chest, and stole her breath. She froze when Leyda cried out again and dug her fingers into the dirt, clawing great chunks out of the ground. She stared down at the ground and gave another cry into the earth, as though she could make the earth itself give Rose back to her again.

Mercy put a hand to her chest, unable to do more than watch. It was horrible to see someone so strong and resilient crumble to pieces. She knew she loved Rose, but she hadn't imagined the depths of that love. And now, it was too late.

Andrei went over to hug Leyda. She wrapped her arms around him, clinging to him like a life raft, desperate for anything to keep her afloat. She wailed into his arms, her cries turning to sobs.

Mercy knew she should do something. She should go over and console her, say something to help, but she couldn't move. Growing up, she was used to hiding when her father had an emotional outburst. Mostly because it involved breaking things. She wasn't sure how to handle someone else crying. She had no experience with that.

After several minutes Leyda calmed again. She ultimately ended up weeping against Andrei's arm. She tried not to let her wrappings fall from her face even as they kept getting wet with tears.

"I'm sorry," Finn whispered, his voice small. He hadn't moved either. Instead he stood looking numb as they all watched Leyda cry. "So many of them go like that. They disappear, they never return, and all we can do is pick up the pieces."

He looked around the camp with a cold, calculating look in his eyes out of place for such a young face.

"Or rather, I guess it's all I can do. Most of them can barely speak anymore let alone help around the camp." He wiped at his eyes, his voice breaking. "I'm really tired."

Mercy took a deep breath and wrapped an arm around herself. She tried to keep her body under control. Leyda was still crying, and it disturbed her—

no, it annoyed her. Mercy had the urge to go over and shake the woman. It was a cruel urge, one that she couldn't understand. That kind of response was uncalled for, so where had it come from? Leyda could shed tears for the woman she loved. She was allowed to hurt. Rose was surely dead by now and they all knew it. So why did Leyda's outburst upset her so much?

Desperate to focus on anything other than Leyda's breakdown, Mercy squatted down and sorted through the basket, pushing aside the cloth that Thomas had stuffed down to cover up everything. Looking around the camp, she realized they had brought far more needles than they needed.

"We have something that might help you all." She glanced to the others who hadn't even responded to Leyda's wail. "At least, we hope it will."

When she pulled the cloth back from the top, Finn gasped and stepped forward. "That's not... Liquid Lead, is it?"

She shook her head. "Something way better than that. I promise."

Finn's eyes went wide as he looked up at her. For the first time since they met, Mercy saw hope there.

"What is it?"

"It's what it isn't that's important. It is not Liquid Lead, and it isn't a full cure."

That hope diminished, but he still looked into the basket as though she carried jewels.

"I call it a partial vaccine. It will turn you human mostly but you can transform at will."

Finn blinked, looking from her to the tiny needles in the basket. "You're kidding me."

She smirked. "No, I'm not." She had expected this reveal to go completely different in her head. It was supposed to take more convincing. She thought Leyda would reveal her face to the pack, confirm who she was, and remind them of the dangers of taking the drug. Yes, it was tested, but not nearly tested enough.

However, Leyda was in no position to help Mercy now. She sat on the opposite end of the fire hugging her knees instead of Andrei. Staring into the fire, she looked not so very different from the rest of the pack. Andrei rubbed her back, clearly trying to help. He looked up and met Mercy's gaze. Mercy nodded toward Finn and he gave a brief nod before getting to his feet to join them.

"Andrei, I thought you could demonstrate what the compound could do for them, seeing as you were the first and only one to test it." She could feel Finn's gaze on her but didn't meet his eyes. It was easier to show them what it would do rather than try to explain it.

"Sure," Andrei said. He shook out his shoulders and put a hand out.

Finn stepped forward as if trying to see through a magic trick.

"Stand back," Andrei warned. "It can get a little messy."

Finn did as he was told.

With a grunt, Andrei's hand split open and fur sprouted out. His claws emerged from his fingertips all while his bones cracked and lengthened. Soon, instead of his normal human hand, a massive werewolf hand sprouted from his human arm, complete with long, sharp claws.

Finn gaped at it. He trembled from head to toe and his eyes were so wide Mercy got worried for him.

"And you don't change at night?" He gulped. Even his voice was shaky.

"Not once in the past six months." Andrei grinned. "Once I transform a limb, it doesn't take much to keep it there. It's just big and cumbersome. When I want to change it back, it takes effort."

He grimaced and focused for a moment before the bones of his hand started cracking again. The fur fell off with the wolf skin attached, revealing beneath it his normal brown skin. The only sign he had done anything —other than the mess at his feet—was a slight blood stain on the end of his shirt sleeve, the perspiration on his arm, and the subtle pinkness of his newly regrown skin. Mercy smiled to herself. He had been practicing.

"I want it," Finn said.

Mercy pulled the basket back slightly. "Okay, but before we give you or the others anything, understand the risks. My friend here is the only one to have successfully been given a dosage. It won't work on a werewolf that's been given Liquid Lead. And the dose can be very painful."

Finn gave a wild laugh and put his arms out, gesturing to the surrounding camp. "Have you seen this place? Do you see how we're living? I know pain. I have felt all forms of it. This miracle drug could be a complete lie for all I care, but if there's a chance it might work, I'll take it. I don't care how painful or dangerous it is. If it means I can try to live a normal life, I don't care. I can't keep living like this. I'm tired of living like an animal."

Andrei folded his arms to join them. "To be honest with you, Finn, I don't know if your friends here will survive it. There's a chance they won't. It could kill them."

Finn raked a hand through his hair and looked around the camp again. Mercy knew he was seeing the squalor, the pain, and the suffering.

"They would probably give their left foot for the chance not to feel like crap any longer. Some of them can't even speak. I have to guess what they need." Finn's gaze swung back to Mercy. "Please. Give them the chance to live a sort of normal life again."

Mercy clenched her jaw and looked to Andrei. This was his camp, or at least, what was left of it. Finn might be too young to make this decision for everyone, but Andrei had seen the camp when it was far better off. He had a better grasp on the group and had more of a right to say what they should do than she did. "What do you think?"

"I mean, it's a risk, but changing every night is a bigger one." He lowered his voice. "These people will die if we don't. Like tonight. I don't know how much time many of them have left. I say do it."

"Leyda?" Mercy called. She was still sitting at the fire with her knees to her chest. "Do you have an opinion?"

Leyda glanced to her, finally acknowledging that she

heard her at least. She cleared her throat then answered in a hoarse voice, "No, I don't."

That familiar anger and frustration rose again, but Mercy tamped it back down. What was wrong with her?

"Fine," she said. "We will do this one at a time and monitor each of them. Finn, if you're okay with it, I'd like to start with you."

Finn nodded and said in a breathy voice, "I'm ready."

MERCY LEANED AGAINST A TREE, listening to an older woman's screams as the partial vaccine ran its course. The sun had traveled far in the sky. They would have to hurry back soon if they hoped to reach Kanta before nightfall.

Finn, Andrei, and Leyda held the woman down to keep her from hurting herself. The doses for the others had gone well, except for the thrashing about after, and it seemed to diminish when Mercy moved away from them. She knew better than to be offended. Her running hypothesis was that the scent of a human being so near drove them wild. She had seen the same thing the night Andrei had been given his dose. Maybe it was more than betrayal she had seen int the wolf's eyes, maybe it was more instinct. The thought made her feel a little better.

It was probably best that Mercy kept her distance from giving out the doses, she decided as she watched. She didn't have the strength others did, and she certainly didn't have the healing capacity if she got injured.

Today had been hard. She admitted that, even though she observed each administered dose with increased fascination. She wished for one of her notebooks so she could get her thoughts down on paper instead of trying to keep it all in her head for later record-keeping.

It was a hard day, but also a rewarding one. She couldn't help but feel pride for the people who would hopefully be on the mend soon. Dosing them wasn't difficult, and neither was holding them down and making sure they were well afterwards. The odd stares as each werewolf gained their mind back made her nervous. She could practically hear their questions even though none of them had voiced it yet.

"Who are these people?"

"What did you do to me?"

"Why is there a human girl here?"

She expected to hear these questions and more after this woman's screams and thrashing died down. She was the last one to get the dosage. Andrei and Leyda might be surprised by them, but she wouldn't be. She had the chance to collect her thoughts, but they did not.

Finally the older woman got to her feet, despite being a little wobbly. Andrei steadied her. He explained for the ninth time what she had been given and what it meant. It was ridiculous how good Andrei was at all of this. He was much better at the bedside manner stuff than Mercy.

Many hugged him. Mercy was grateful he was

willing to do the emotional work. She was sure she would have said something callous if she were hugged by so many strangers back to back, but Andrei seemed to enjoy it. The two of them were very different people, yet they complemented each other so well.

She didn't mind hugs from Andrei or Thomas, or even sometimes Leyda, but a bunch of strangers was too much. Mercy couldn't remember her father ever hugging her as a child, though she was certain it had happened at some point.

Mercy stepped forward and gestured to the knapsack Andrei had dropped near the bonfire. "I'm afraid it's late and we have to get going."

Voices rose in confusion and reluctance, but Mercy continued. They didn't have time to argue.

"You'll find food, water, clothes, and money in the bag. Consider it a way to jump-start your new lives. We thought there would be more of you, so there should be plenty. I recommend bathing first before going into any town. We can't help you beyond this. Good luck to all of you."

Mercy gestured toward the path and Andrei hurried over to her side.

"Do you think it's a good idea to just leave them like this? I doubt this is the only werewolf camp in these woods. Come nightfall they could get hurt. Maybe we should take them back with us?"

Leyda trailed behind Andrei, her eyes distant as though the spark had gone out of them. It was strange to see her so quiet.

"We don't have a choice," Mercy said. "There is no

safe place to take them that won't cause suspicion. Can you imagine us trying to walk them through Kanta and back to the factory? We would cause immediate suspicion and I don't know what would happen to them. At least here in thew woods they have a chance. They will just have to defend themselves come nightfall."

He shook his head with a sigh. "You're right, I just hate it. We do so much, but it never feels like it's enough."

Someone rushed up behind them. Mercy made a concerted effort not to turn around, but then Finn called out.

"Wait! Hold up, before you go. Please?"

Andrei took her hand and pulled her back. He chuckled under his breath. She bit back a retort.

Finn stood with his eyes wide and glassy. He had been practicing his transformations in between helping with the doses. Clearly he still intended to be the group's guardian. It was actually kind of sweet.

"How can we ever thank you for this? I don't even know where you're from." He gave a nervous laugh and raked a hand through his hair.

"You don't have to do anything," Andrei said. Mercy could hear the smile in his voice. It always melted her heart despite her best intentions. "Just get out of this place and live well. Be safe. And most importantly, keep your werewolf side hidden. We can't let anyone know what we're doing. If any of you reveal that you can transform, the hunting will start all over again. For all of us."

Finn huffed and gave a nervous nod. Then he

lunged forward and hugged Andrei so tight that Mercy wondered if he had trouble breathing. Andrei's eyes grew misty as he hugged him back.

Leyda stared for a moment before turning away from them.

"Be safe, okay?" Andrei said, "Be happy."

Finn pulled away and wiped at his eyes with his dirty sleeve. "Thank you, Andrei."

Mercy crouched down in front of him, grateful for Leyda's expertise with the wrappings that ensured she could not be seen or recognized. "You can't share our names with anyone either. It's too dangerous and might put us and our work at risk. But if you run into other werewolves who are struggling, you can tell them we are the Wolves of Kanta. We hunt the real monsters."

His face lit up, and he nodded. "I'll tell them."

"They can send a letter to Kanta," Andrei added. "Directed to the Wolves of Kanta. We'll get them."

Mercy smiled up at him.

"Thank you," he said. "I'll find them and tell them so they can get help too. I promise."

Leyda started walking down the path back toward Kanta. For the first time that day, Mercy agreed with her.

She got to her feet and turned toward the path. Andrei slipped his hand into hers again and she gave it a squeeze.

One werewolf camp down, far too many to go.

AUTUMN'S ARRIVAL meant the days were getting shorter but weren't as short as winter yet. Mercy was grateful they didn't have to sprint back to Kanta like the last time they came. With just a casual walking pace, they made it back to the edge of town by dusk.

Mercy took a moment to catch her breath as Andrei and Leyda waited with her. This time Leyda didn't give her any trouble, not a single word about having to wait. Her attitude had changed completely since their journey to the camp.

The small town of Kanta lay beyond the treeline. A pair of dirt roads cut through the center of it and the wooden buildings bordered them. Already she could see candlelight and hearths flickering inside, lighting up the buildings. It was beautiful, she thought, especially now that the woods were a little safer than they had been the night before.

"We made it!" Andrei laughed, finally relaxed enough to talk again. "I admit, I was worried. I didn't expect it to take so long. We'll have to consider that when we come across the larger camps."

Leyda nodded, "Yes, you two will need to plan ahead next time. That could have ended very differently."

Mercy exchanged a worried look with Andrei. "What do you mean?" She turned toward her. "You'll be with us next time, won't you?"

"No, I won't." She paused and clamped her hands together tight in front of her. "I don't think I have the stomach for this."

Mercy gaped at her. After those long speeches Leyda

had given her last year, she no longer had the stomach for this? Did she expect Andrei to hold the transforming werewolves down on his own? Now that she knew Rose wasn't waiting for her, she bowed out.

"Oh, come on, don't talk like that," Andrei urged, probably sensing the rising tension. "You're just upset, that's all. Besides, I'll still need your help holding them down after—"

"I think you're more than capable of doing that yourself," she whispered. "I can't do what you all do. It's… different now. I don't have it in me any longer. The only ties I had to that forsaken place were to Rose, and now she—" She went silent and dropped her head, drawing herself inward. "I just can't."

Andrei put a hand on her shoulder.

Mercy's hands shook. Her pulse raced, and she locked her teeth together to keep the rage under wraps. Instead of unleashing on her, Mercy took a deep breath of the crisp air.

Finally she asked, "What will you do then?"

"Continue my work at the mill. There are many like me who still need my help, trapped between forms, unable to move forward or back. I'll continue to help them."

All three were briefly silent before Andrei dared to tack on, "Until Mercy comes up with a cure to fix all of you, right? Then you'll be like me and the other werewolves."

Leyda closed her eyes and Mercy briefly wondered if she was struggling with her anger as much as Mercy.

Leyda unclasped her hands and instead balled her fists at her sides before heading down the slope toward town.

"She doesn't think I can do it," Mercy hissed to Andrei as they headed down a good distance behind her.

"I think she's grieving. She had a rough day, is all."

Mercy shook her head and held his arm for a moment, holding them back, afraid Leyda could still hear her. "No, she said she doesn't have the stomach for this. That was a message to me. She told me that when I couldn't watch Carter's first werewolf transformation."

Andrei put a hand on her shoulder. "Don't you think you're reading into things? I think she's still broken up about Rose. You saw what happened."

Mercy shook her head and looked down through the trees where she could see Leyda walking down the street toward the mill. "I think she's angry. She hated that I made a cure for you and not for her. Remember?"

"Yeah, but—"

"I think losing Rose just gave her another reason to be angry at me. That's the real reason she doesn't want to help with the next camp. She wants me to give her a cure too. As though it's that simple."

Andrei sighed and took her hand, leading her down the hill to town. "I think you've been spending too much time in that laboratory, Mercy. Not everything is about you. Let the woman grieve."

Mercy winced. That one stung.

4

THE TORTOISE

A COLD WIND **BLEW** leaves down to scrape across the floor of grinder number nine. Autumn had come with a vengeance, bringing with it cold days and colder nights along with a beautiful array of colors.

Mercy sat on the catwalk, letting her legs hang between the bars of the banister, her feet swinging back and forth as she watched Thomas work below. Grinder number nine was the farthest away from the intake room, and the least likely to be interrupted by unwanted guests.

On a normal day, the grinder moved steadily along, no longer powered by unwilling, armless werewolves, but by Thomas' new steam engine, which pulled power from the bellows below. Thomas's design was far more efficient than the normal steam engine trains that tore through the landscape. It took a fraction of the energy of a train's steam engine to run this grinder, and he assured her that all of Farrell Mill would run seamlessly on less than what it took to move a train. Grinder number nine was the first prototype to be installed.

Thomas was far more of a genius with mechanical gears, pulleys, and steam than with vials, chemicals, and Bunsen burners. Mercy had quickly learned chemistry was more her area of specialty, much to her surprise. Her father would have balked at her working with chemicals day in and day out. Then again, he would have never let her work in Farrell Mill. He saw it as a dangerous place, even though hunting werewolves was hardly any safer.

Down below, people filed out the back door, carrying gifted bundles with them. The last time Mercy saw these people, they were trapped in cages, snarling and biting at anyone who came past. Today they were living outside of a cage. They had volunteered to take her partial cure, to take a chance at a new life, and were being given a fresh start.

A teenage boy only a few years older than her looked up to the catwalk. He shielded his eyes from the morning sun. Once he spotted her, he gasped and turned to an older man beside him. He tapped him on the shoulder and the teen pointed up to where Mercy sat.

She stopped swinging her legs on instinct. Her face grew hot, and a frown formed on her lips. Why were they staring at her? She purposely had dressed in baggy clothes to hide her shape and as high up as she was, they wouldn't be able to tell if she was a man or a woman. Thank goodness for the long ladder that separated them.

The older man must have been the teen's father. They had a similar gait. The realization made a tightness form in her chest. The teen waved up at her, all smiles, and the older man waved too. Her heart jumped to her throat. What was wrong with them? Why were they waving at her like she was some kind of benefactor? She was just loitering on the catwalk, minding her own business and watching the people below. The ultimate shock came when the pair clasped hands and bowed to her.

Mercy grunted in surprise and shook her head. Then an uncomfortable realization fell over her. Were they thanking her?

Reluctantly she lifted a hand and gave a weak wave back at them, unsure how else to respond. Somehow Thomas had to be the cause of this. Was he telling them who she was? Did he put this weird idea into their head?

She spotted Thomas' bright red hair as he made his way across the grounds. He spoke with the pair, passing over bundles he carried in his arms. Each bundle had clothes, money, and identification so they could live a normal life. Leyda would drive them wherever they wanted, as long as they could reach it on half a day's ride and it was outside of Kanta.

The teenager wrapped Thomas in a hug and Mercy's eyes stung with tears. No, she didn't need that. She took a deep breath and forced herself to watch as Thomas led them over to the exterior door he had put in during renovations. The father shook Thomas' hand with such vigor Mercy chuckled. If Thomas' arm wasn't mechanical, he would have likely winced.

Thankfully the father and son were the last ones in today's group, and Mercy climbed to her feet and reached for the ladder.

It had been a week since their visit to the werewolf camp, a week since she had spoken to Leyda, and a week of waiting on Thomas to help the cured werewolves start their new lives. There were too many of them to send out on their own all at once. She understood that, but still, she hated having to wait to speak with Thomas. Of course, she could have spoken to him with the partially cured werewolves too, but that took more effort than Mercy could muster. When she was at the mill, she tried not to have to wear the face wrappings. Instead, she waited until Thomas had closed the door before she climbed to her feet.

She gripped the cold metal ladder and started down. They had a lot to talk about.

"I'M glad to see you out of the laboratory, Mercy. It's been days, hasn't it?" Thomas greeted her as her boots hit the gravel floor.

He was smiling but clearly tired. She could see the exhaustion creeping into the bags beneath his eyes and the crinkles of his smile. He hadn't even bothered to put on his fur-lined cape today, and Mercy couldn't remember the last time she saw him without it.

"Andrei said I was spending too much time down there, so I took a break for a bit. Stretch my legs, get to see what other work was going on around the mill."

"Oh, is that it?" He flipped open the panel on his right arm to tweak some gears within. Maybe the werewolf father had shaken his hand harder than she thought. "I assumed you were holing yourself up because we had so much company for the last week. I know you're not fond of that."

She shrugged, unable to suppress a smile. "Yeah, I guess that's true too."

He flipped the hatch closed and allowed his fingers to twitch one by one. He must have had to reset them. "So, what's on your mind? You come here every morning to watch people start their new lives after being given your cure, but this is the first time you've come down to talk. It must be important."

Her smile went thin. Thomas' personality was sometimes abrasive, making her laugh one minute and feel silly the next. "Those last two. They acted like they knew who I was. Did you see them bow to me?"

He shot a look at her, his lazy eye a little slower to catch up. "They bowed to you? That's a little odd…"

"I think someone told them about me, and I don't like that. I don't want any of them to know who cured them. The more attention drawn to me, the more difficult it is for me to hide here."

"I agree. This situation is dangerous enough as it is. I can assure you I haven't told them hardly anything. The only other people who could have spoken to them… Hmm, let's see. Only Andrei and Leyda have been near any of them. None of the workers below are permitted close to the tower, so it would have to be one of them."

Mercy slid her eyes closed and tried to calm the

anger that threatened to overwhelm her. Leyda. It had to be her. Was that why she volunteered to take the partially cured werewolves to their new homes to begin with? Had she wanted to put Mercy's life in danger from the start? She could remember the sad "Happy Birthday" Leyda had said to her last year. She seemed truly sorry not to be closer to her. How quickly that mindset had shifted once Mercy created the first partial cure that wasn't for Leyda.

Thomas seemed to come to the same conclusion she had. "I can speak with Leyda. I'm sure she didn't mean to put you at risk. These people are grateful to you. If it slipped, then I'm sure no harm was intended."

"Would you please stop making excuses for her?" The words had sprung to her lips with almost a life of their own.

Thomas sighed and rubbed at the bridge of his nose. "I don't mean to make excuses. I just wish you two would get along like you used to."

"Like when you both planned to turn me into a werewolf against my will? I wouldn't call that getting along."

He shook his head. "Mercy…"

"I know, that's too far. I'm sorry." She walked a few paces around the grinder, along the same path the chained werewolves used to take. Her boots crunched dried leaves into the gravel. "Ever since the night I transformed Andrei, things haven't been the same between us. I thought we could remain friends despite the cure not working for her. I thought we could still work together, as professionals if nothing else. But then at the camp, that fell apart too."

"Rose left. Yes, she told me."

Mercy ground a leaf into pieces with her boot. "Regardless of how much she dislikes me or hates me for not making a cure for her, I can't let her put our lives in danger. If she did it to me, she might have done it to Andrei too." She gestured toward the closed back door. "Sure, those people you help may mean well, but people talk. I don't want attention drawn to the only girl at Farrell Mill, you know what I mean?"

Thomas stepped around, then put a hand on her shoulder. She turned away from the dried leaves and turned to him.

"I've been thinking of that lately," he said, his voice filled with concern. "I worry about you and Andrei heading to the camp in Crowsmirth on your own together. Leyda's disguises are good to keep your identities a secret, but people will talk if they see you leaving the mill repeatedly with your basket of needles. Crowsmirth is crawling with hunters if this latest werewolf delivery is any indication. If you two go there—are recognized as the same ones always coming to and from the mill—people will pick up on patterns. After some time, the cured werewolves will impact the hunters too. They will suspect."

She shrugged. "Isn't that good though? If we make such a big dent on the werewolf population that hunters notice, won't that be seen as positive? Surely people want to see fewer werewolf attacks."

He gave a small, sad smile. "Some do, of course. But

not all. You two will be seen as taking away employment from werewolf hunters. Talk has already begun. Hunters have come to me all week complaining. They believe the werewolves of Kanta just disappeared overnight. No attacks, no trails, not even any glimpsed in the forest. Yes, there are howls at night, but from what I've heard, no werewolves have been spotted. One man let his whole pack of dogs stay in the woods overnight. All of them came back the next day unscathed."

Mercy flung her arms out to her sides. "That's great! Why are they even complaining about that?"

"Because they see it as a bad omen. This is how they make money, Mercy. This is how they put food on the table."

She pulled away from him. "I don't get it. Can't they go back to whatever they did before hunting were-wolves? Can't they just go back to catching rabbits or whatever?"

"Werewolves have lived in these forests for over ten years. Do you really think there are many other profes-sions left here in Kanta?"

She crossed her arms. "No, but——"

"What about your father? Would he be satisfied with doing anything other than hunting werewolves?"

Clenching her jaw, she sighed. Thomas was right. Mercy's father would have been offended at the recom-mendation of trying a different career path. Being a werewolf hunter was as much his identity as becoming a werewolf hunter had been part of hers. It was a point of pride now instead of a mere profession.

"You know I hate it when you're right."

He chuckled and extended his arm around her shoulders. "And I get so focused on making a point that sometimes I'm careless of the damage I make along the way. I'm sorry to bring up Solomon, but my point is that we could accidentally make many enemies if we're not careful."

Mercy narrowed her eyes at him. She had been so wrapped up in his words she had missed the obvious. Thomas was exhausted, yes, but it was like when he made a new invention. He was also terrible at beating around the bush when he could just say what was on his mind.

"You've done something, haven't you?"

Thomas's laughter was spontaneous, like the bubbling sound of a child struggling to keep a secret. How had she missed it before?

"You may have taken over the chemicals at Farrell Mill, Mercy, but I still maintain the mechanical experiments."

He rubbed his hands together as he led her to the ladder. Maybe Andrei was right, she thought as Thomas careened up the rings of the ladder with his powerful arms. Maybe she had spent far too much time in the laboratory.

IN HER ALMOST TWO years of living at the mill, Mercy had never gone down into the tunnels beneath the tower. They weren't just more floors of the tower, like she might have expected. Instead they extended out in winding paths like an underground ant colony beneath the grinders.

The air was hot and humid, completely disregarding the chilly temperatures above ground. It smelled like coal and tickled the back of her throat. Furnaces burned constantly beneath each grinder and Mercy understood why Thomas had insisted she wear her wrappings down here. While the grinders no longer required manual werewolf labor, the grain still needed to be sifted before spilling into the grinders. The furnaces needed to be kept at a low, steady heat to supply steam for the conveyor belts and gears. Workers ran back and forth through the narrow stone hallways lit by meek oil lanterns that fussed and swung along the ceiling. Aboveground the grinders appeared to work like magic, but down here was where the magic was made.

"My father built these tunnels," Thomas said, as they hugged the wall. A man with a wheelbarrow of coal pushed quickly past with barely a glance to Thomas or Mercy. "His focus was more on making money rather than innovation. Much of this used to be run from a water wheel, but a town up north dammed up the river years ago. It almost destroyed us."

He ducked to avoid a hanging lantern. He paused as the hall curved to the right and stopped at one of the many wooden doors built into the stone walls. He pulled out an old keyring, fit one key into a large brass keyhole. When the door swung open, brilliant afternoon light filled the tunnel and Mercy had to shield her eyes from it. The light exposed the rough-hewn stone walls and floor, how dim the oil lanterns were, and how everything was covered in black soot.

On down the hall, a fire roared as something was thrown into one of the furnaces, and a black cloud emerged, forcing her to cough as she stumbled outside into the light.

Thomas pushed the door closed behind them before patting her on the back. She coughed a while longer before it finally subsided.

"That was terrible! How do they even breathe down there?"

"Oh, um..." Thomas hesitated as though he had never considered the question of air before. "I don't actually know, now that you mention it. I guess it is rather terrible to smell all the time."

Mercy shook her head, still clearing her throat. "You mean you can build mechanical grinders and mechanical arms, but you can't help any of your own workers?" She jutted a thumb over her shoulder.

"Please, I came here to show you what I made for you, not to be chastised—*again*—for overlooking some silly work ethic issue."

She grumbled, "Maybe if you had a better work ethic, I wouldn't have to complain so much."

Thomas stepped aside and gestured behind him. It took Mercy a moment to take in everything.

They stood inside a cave, only the sides of it had been carved out by hand instead of Mother Nature. The other end of the cave opened to the sky and an enormous water wheel. She stepped closer, drawn to the structure almost as big as one of Thomas's grinders. As she drew nearer, she realized how old it was. The paddles on the wheel were warped and bleached, from spending too many years in the sun and far too few years in the water as intended. Water shoots that would normally direct the water inside to power machinery were cut off, leaving only the wheel behind. She leaned out of the cave, examining where the old water trough used to extend.

"Careful," Thomas warned. "That's a steep drop."

Mercy glanced down. He was right. Because of the field of yellowed grass that extended out below it was hard to tell a river ever poured through at first glance, but there were a few indicators of its past size. The walls of the cliff were smooth rock, and the ground dipped on the opposite bank. Had the river once extended out that far? It was strange to imagine Kanta as a river town, but that made far more sense than it being a trapper town— or the home of so many werewolf hunters.

"Who had the river dammed?" she asked, feeling suddenly sad to see the empty field of grass instead of an active, rushing river that had clearly been big and formidable back in the day.

"Rumors said the wealthy lords up north paid Kanta's mayor a small fortune for it. They wanted more water resources for themselves, so they took our river."

Mercy shook her head. "I didn't know we even had a mayor."

He smiled, "After it was finished, the lords took the fortune made off of Kanta's water and the mayor disappeared. Technically he is still mayor because of some loophole he put into place, but nobody knows what happened to him. He could have been turned into a werewolf for all we know." He shrugged, "So yes, Kanta has a mayor officially, but not really."

"That's ridiculous," Mercy snapped. "He shouldn't be allowed to be mayor if he's too cowardly to even show his face."

Thomas chuckled. "I do love how you voice your opinion so succinctly!" He cleared his throat. "Come see what I made for you."

She turned. With chagrin, she realized she had walked right past Thomas's work table. On a bookshelf sat a dozen mechanical arms, all at various stages of completion. Some were incredibly simple and generic, while others were so realistic and sophisticated she could have believed they were real arms.

"Wow, you made all of these?" She reached out to stroke the finger of one. It felt cold but she could feel the ridges in its fingertip. It was almost uncanny the amount of detail Thomas put into these.

"Yes, those are all mine. From my very first at the top, to my latest invention at the bottom. I've been trying to build more to prepare for if—for when we get a cure for the werewolves that used to be on the grinders. If they aren't able to grow back their limbs, well, at least I'll have an alternative." He clasped his hands together and bounced on his toes. "That still isn't what I wanted to show you, Mercy."

His lazy eye gave him away like it always did. She followed it to the center of his workbench. They looked like two metallic wolf heads. She moved in closer.

"Thomas, what are these?"

"You and Andrei need disguises, and I mean more than what a few tattered bandages can provide. That's not practical when you're dealing with life-threatening situations. They could fall off, they're a fire risk… I could go on and on about the dangers. When you are away on a mission, I can hire people to dress up as you, to walk around Kanta and cover for your absence. I can protect you here, but I can't protect you when you leave."

She picked up one of the heads. It was small and surprisingly lightweight. Although it felt like it was made of metal, it was lighter and more flexible. Turning it in the light, she examined the light gray color of the metal. The craftsmanship was exquisite, not that she was surprised.

Thomas took the wolf's head from her and fit it over her head. "Andrei told me you call yourselves the Wolves of Kanta. I figured you may as well look the part."

Thomas had put padding down at the base of the neck and on top of the shoulders. What she had assumed to be the wolf's eyes was really a single plated visor that could slide down to shield her eyes and her identity.

"The green lenses are on both models. They will be useful in both broad daylight and at dusk when you may want them. They will help you see dark shadows and prevent glare. I think it will also be a jarring enough disguise to shock people enough that they shouldn't cause you too much trouble."

He pulled a few straps looser, tightened a few others, and soon Mercy was practicing flipping the visor up and down, watching herself in a polished metal strip that Thomas used as a mirror.

"What do you think?" he asked.

"I love it! I'm so glad I don't have to wear those smelly bandages anymore."

"Now, don't get too excited." He held up a hand, smiling at her enthusiasm. "You'll still need to wear the wrappings in and around Kanta. Any place you're likely to be among normal people, anytime you want to blend, that's when you want the normal disguise. Otherwise all of this will be for nothing. The helmet, however, should be used when you're in the woods and might face a hunter on their territory."

She slid the visor up. "Thank you, Thomas. I mean it. This is amazing."

He smiled. "Thank you. Now before you go, I wanted to show you one more thing. This way."

Leading to the end of the cave, Thomas turned and shimmied to the side. Mercy followed him nervously, still wearing the wolf's head. "Thomas?"

A hand emerged from beside the water wheel, gesturing for her to approach. She did and found a small ledge only a couple of feet wide beside the wheel.

"Watch your step," he warned. "Here, give me your hand."

She did, careful of her footing as she shuffled behind Thomas. The thin ledge curved back along the outer curve of the cave and then got wider. She couldn't have possibly seen it from inside the cave, but out here she saw the path was wide enough to be a road.

Clinging to Thomas and the wall, she finally made

it. She spread her legs out and stopped to catch her breath.

"Hey, you okay?"

Up ahead, Andrei leaned against the wall, seemingly not bothered by the drop. She hadn't seen him come in, so he must have been here before they arrived. She was a little worried about him not wearing any wrappings out here, but of course, nobody could see anything on this ledge. The sheer cliff face meant nobody could climb up to the cave or the ledge. Even down in the grassy field, nobody could make out much from below. Not even a werewolf could climbed a vertical wall up to this height.

Beside Andrei sat a vehicle that looked very odd. It looked different from the other vehicles Thomas owned. Riveted metal covered all sides and she couldn't tell if it was here for repair or if Thomas had made alterations to it.

She turned to Andrei with a smile. "You mean he told you about this before me?"

Andrei glanced to Thomas then back to her, rubbing the back of his neck. "Honestly? I wasn't sure if you were ready yet. You've been wound up tight about your experiments ever since we got back from the camp. I thought you needed a break."

Anger reared its head, but Mercy pushed it down. Andrei was right. She hadn't been ready. Despite Leyda's attempted backstabbing, Mercy couldn't throw herself completely into her work day in and day out. She could lose herself to it.

She stood up and asked, "Okay, I'm ready now.

What is this?" She gestured to the vehicle.

Andrei chuckled and Thomas grinned. Had Andrei been helping him with this? If so, that was wonderful news. She wanted Andrei to have friends beyond herself.

Thomas turned to the vehicle. "I thought you would never ask." He patted the side of the vehicle that reminded her of her father's modified truck now that she got a better view of it.

"The truck itself is modular in design, built to be whatever you need it to be. Are you doing a search and rescue mission? Or a werewolf capture perhaps? The floor of the truck bed comes out to carry several werewolf cages at a time." He turned with a smirk, "I took your father's original idea and expanded it to suite our needs."

Mercy blinked in shock. "That's amazing."

"But what truly gives the truck its name is its defensible properties. Andrei, do you mind demonstrating?"

"Sure!" He pulled out five heavy slabs of metal from the truck bed and moved around the vehicle, dropping the metal slabs into the ground so that they stood up at odd angles.

"The truck bed is modular too, and can be configured into a defensible position. A net can be thrown over the car and fit easily into the slots of the metal sheets, like Andrei is demonstrating now. And with a simple pull of a lever, the metal is electrified."

Andrei pulled a lever inside the car and instantly the entire metal shell lit up with electricity. Mercy gasped, unable to keep from backing away from the light and shower of sparks.

"This is powerful enough to knock out a werewolf, but won't kill them. Let's say you're fending off oh, five werewolves. It will fend them off beautifully. More than that and it could short-circuit, so be certain of what you're facing should you need to use it." Thomas stared at the charged field with pure glee in his eyes. "More importantly, if any foolish hunters try to shoot at it, they will wish they hadn't."

Mercy stared at him for a long moment after Thomas remained silent. She rolled her eyes. He could be infuriating sometimes. "Okay," she prodded, "then what will it do to them? Will it kill them?"

His lazy eye rolled toward her. "It will send out an electric arc in the gunshot's direction. It quite honestly could kill them, I have no idea. I imagine they would only try it once. Regardless, the Tortoise should keep you both safe should you need to spend an evening in the forest alone—regardless of what is after you."

Mercy arched her eyebrows as Andrei shut off the electrical current. "The Tortoise?"

Thomas smiled and glanced to Andrei.

"Yeah!" Andrei said excitedly. "Get it? 'Cause it has a protective shell?" He kicked the metal plating, causing a ding. "It's fun to drive too, Mercy! I'm sure you'll be a natural after a bit."

Mercy shook her head, not sure what she had gotten herself into. The Wolves of Kanta now rode around in an electrified tortoise and it made absolutely no sense. But she couldn't possibly say no to it. It would make driving up to Crowsmirth feel much safer. Besides, she hadn't seen Andrei so excited about something in ages, and definitely not so early in the morning.

"So what's your verdict?" Thomas asked.

"It's dangerous, deadly, has a terrible name, and I don't have a clue how to even drive the damn thing…" She shrugged, "Sure, why not? It's sure better than being sitting ducks in the woods between Crowsmirth and Kanta, praying for dawn to come save us."

Andrei threw his hands up into the air, "See? I told you she would love it! And she doesn't like the name, but she doesn't want to change it either. I consider that a win. I am clearly awesome at picking names."

Thomas laughed and shook his head. "And I consider that a loss. Whoever heard of naming a car after such a notoriously slow animal like a tortoise? That's hardly a worthwhile name for such a genius creation!"

Mercy laughed. Now this was an argument worth having, and she had no plans of stepping in to stop it.

PART 2

THE CITY OF CROWS

5

____

LEAVING KANTA

DIRT KICKED UP behind the tires as Andrei drove them through the streets of Kanta on a crisp, clear October morning. Mercy lay one arm against the window as the cool wind blew across her face, tossing the ties of her wrappings behind her. People gave them nervous looks as drove by. Regardless of the good they did, the people of Kanta were terrified of them, and probably always would be.

Mercy wasn't sure if it was because of the metal monstrosity they drove down the street, affectionately called The Tortoise despite Thomas' protests, or if it was because of the disguises they wore. Though in retrospect, Kanta was unwelcome to anyone who looked different. She had learned that when she accompanied her father into town years ago. No, it was more than just their outfits or their vehicle. It was because it clearly marked them as coming from the mill. To the people of Kanta, they were nameless strangers hired to do any kind of unspeakable act at the request of Thomas

Farrell. They didn't see the good done, the lives saved, or the potential deaths they prevented.

If only they could put aside their prejudices about werewolves, maybe then Mercy and Andrei could explain their true mission. Maybe then there would be less fear of them. Of course, Mercy knew the odds of that were near impossible.

"You can't let it get to you," Andrei said, his voice muffled by his own cloth wrappings. Even as he said this, he glanced in the direction of the apothecary on the back road, barely visible between the gap between the pub and the store. "They don't understand what we're doing. I don't think they would approve even if they did."

He turned back to the road, but Mercy saw the way he gripped the steering wheel tighter.

"It makes you angry," she said. It wasn't a question but an observation.

Andrei sighed. "Trust me, I want nothing more than to run into that shop, hug old Mr. Winters, and tell him how much I've missed him. But I know what he saw at my house, what happened to the rest of my family. He would suspect what I was and even if I explained it to him, I would have to be afraid of him the entire time, knowing he might kill me."

The Tortoise left Kanta behind in a dust cloud. They shifted onto the more overgrown road that led to Crowsmirth. It made Mercy sad to know Andrei could never reconnect with his old friends. It also made her angry that people allowed themselves to be consumed by fear.

"Maybe he wasn't really a friend to begin with," she offered. "Maybe you're better off without him."

Andrei opened his mouth and glanced to her, but instead of speaking, he reached over and squeezed her hand.

"I'll be honest, Mercy—" He was interrupted by the wheels going over a cluster of rocks before he continued. "Sometimes you scare the hell out of me when you talk like that."

She narrowed her eyes. "Why? Because your old boss would shoot you even if you promised you weren't dangerous anymore? That doesn't sound like a real friend, even if he was frightened. I know that doesn't sound nice, but it's true."

Andrei pursed his lips. "He has a right to be scared. You can't just push people away because they disagree with you."

"Disagreeing with me is way different from trying to kill my boyfriend. You're being too nice about it. If you came to me and told me you weren't a werewolf anymore, do you think I would try to kill you to confirm it? Or do you think I would ask questions?"

He dragged a hand across his cheek, picking at a stray piece of fabric. "No, but you're different!"

"I'm sorry, but you can't call someone a friend if they try to kill you. That's not how it works."

They both went silent and Mercy listened to the wheels as they crunched over dirt and gravel, following the same tire tracks etched out by every other vehicle that came down this road. The line of weeds between the tire tracks disappeared under the hood of the car.

She wondered if her father had ever driven up to Crowsmirth. Not that he would have ever told her let alone taken her with him. He had kept her so sheltered as a child. She had seen so little.

"What about Leyda?" Andrei asked.

"What?" Mercy's thoughts were so off track, she wasn't sure what he meant.

"She was going to have you bitten and turned into a werewolf at Thomas' request. Without your cure, that's practically a death sentence. Yet you two still work together. Do you consider her a friend still?"

He made a good point. Leyda had wanted her to be turned into a werewolf, it was true, and partly because at the time she wanted Mercy to pay for the wrongs done against her. Mercy's father had been the hunter to bring Leyda in to Farrell Mill and indirectly caused her to have her arms removed. Leyda remembered it. On one hand Mercy understood her rage, but on the other it felt wrong to take out that rage on the child of her target. Then again, Mercy had been following in her father's footsteps. She had wanted to be a hunter.

"She and I have a complicated relationship," Mercy finally answered.

"I mean clearly," he said with a short laugh. "I thought you two were going to kill each other when we went to the camp. More like she would kill you." He shook his head. "I laugh, but I was a little worried."

"We used to be friends, or at least close to it. But now..." She shook her head. "Now, I don't know what we are anymore."

He reached over and took her hand again. "I'm

sorry, I don't mean to push. It's difficult. I guess I can't quite give up on my old life yet, even though I should have buried those feelings a long time ago. Sometimes that was the only thing that got me through the day, back at the camp. As crazy as it sounds, I don't know if I'll ever give up on that."

She smiled at him. "If it means that much to you, I'm sorry. Don't let a jerk like me take away your hope. Besides, there's a great big world out there outside of Kanta. Maybe you could still work at an apothecary somewhere."

He perked up at that. "I could imagine us owning a shop together, you know that? You and I selling normal wares by day, and administering werewolf vaccines by night. I would like that."

"I like that idea." She brought his hand up to put a light kiss on the back of his hand through the wrappings. He squirmed in his seat and glanced her way.

"Hey, you're my jerk." He squeezed her hand affectionately. Then pulled his hand back to navigate a bend in the road. "Don't forget that, okay?"

Mercy felt her face get hot and cuddled closer to him on the patchwork leather seat. "And you're my werewolf," she whispered.

He gave a nervous laugh and his left leg started jumping. Mercy grinned. It was fun to torment him when he couldn't do anything about it. How much she wanted to wrap her arms around him and hug him, but she didn't want to distract his driving. They had no time for that. It didn't seem like there was ever enough time. For now she would just have to be satisfied with making him a nervous driver and stealing kisses when she could.

She hoped Andrei knew how much she loved him because sometimes it was easier to joke and make innuendos than it was to say what she meant. Words alone couldn't convey what she really felt.

The Tortoise rolled on, winding along the worn dirt road around thick woods and skirting beneath great limbs of ancient trees. Every moment put more distance between them and Kanta and that suited Mercy just fine. She felt freer when leaving town, even if it was just for a day.

THE CITY of Crowsmirth was aptly named. As soon as they approached the city and saw the first buildings in the distance, it seemed like every tree they passed was filled with crows. It was kind of unnerving to see their eyes watching them as they drove toward town. Mercy came to Crowsmirth, bracing herself to deal with werewolves not the beady-eyed watchers in the trees or the flocks flying up overhead.

An enormous flock emerged out of the trees and briefly made the road disappear in front of them. "Is this normal?"

For a moment all they could see were a cloud of black birds and the air was filled with caws and the beating of wings. Andrei gasped, hitting the brake on reflex, and Mercy froze. Then just as quick as they appeared, the crows disappeared into the forest on the other side of the road.

Andrei's hands shook on the wheel and he was taking deep breaths. They had been driving for hours, but they hadn't seen a single car come from the opposite direction, or even one come up behind them from Kanta. He had mentioned it was unusual a few minutes ago, but now the strangeness felt like a warning. Mercy had the distinct feeling that coming to Crowsmirth was a bad idea, but what choice did they have? This was the risk they took by chasing werewolf packs.

"We used to come here to trade for supplies," Andrei said with a shaky voice. "We had shipments every day. I used to drive down every morning, five days a week. In the years I worked there, I never saw this road so empty." He slowed the car down as they approached the buildings of downtown Crowsmirth.

As they slowly rolled closer, Mercy knew something terrible had happened here.

Crowsmirth was smaller than Kanta with only a single wide road for downtown. Buildings lined the entire length of the road, giving it a horseshoe shape. Stores were in front. Smaller homes stood behind the buildings where the people likely lived. Mercy felt the hairs go up on her arms. The store windows were open with broken shutters hanging from the window frames. Shattered wooden doors sat in the middle of the street. Despite being made of heavy, thick wood, they had been torn to pieces. Pools of blood puddled on the empty street and that seemed to be a big draw for the massive amounts of crows that had descended on the city.

Birds everywhere, cawed and flapped their wings, covering almost the entire street. More birds joined the massive numbers from the trees. A black swarm of them settled down toward the front near their vehicle.

The most perplexing was that there were no bodies in sight, just puddles of blood, as though the clouds had poured blood onto the streets overnight. Almost every puddle was surrounded by crows. Mercy shuddered.

At first she thought of the pools of blood she had seen at the werewolf camp near Kanta, but this was a town where people lived. No werewolves would live so close to a human civilization. The danger would be too great.

If this was human blood, then where were the bodies? What happened to them? Curiosity clawed at Mercy and she glanced to her basket of needles. They came here to investigate the werewolf camp, to understand what was going on so they could help. This was part of it, it had to be.

Mercy gestured to Andrei whose hands were still trembling. "Can you stop up here?"

"*Stop?* Why?" His opinion was clear. This was not a good place to stop, but Mercy had to know what was happening. They were here to help werewolves, and this place clearly knew them well. Andrei's eyes darted from her to the desolate scene before them. "It's too dangerous, we can't stop here."

"I need to find out what happened. If there are any werewolves here, we need to help them."

Andrei pulled the car over, just a short way off the road, but a good distance away from the buildings. He could easily get back on the street again if he had to. "I'll keep it running until you get back."

Mercy hopped down and turned back to him. "You can't tell if it's werewolf or human blood, can you?"

He gave a nervous laugh. "You've got to be joking. There are way too many scents out here for me to discern anything." Reaching behind his seat, he pulled out a shotgun not too different from the rifle he used when he guarded the werewolf camp.

Mercy reached into her seat and pulled out a few empty vials. Another benefit of having the Tortoise with them was she could bring as much laboratory equipment as she wanted. There was plenty of space for it.

She hopped out, the sound of her feet hitting the gravel almost echoing. She took a deep breath of the crisp air to calm herself. Closing the door behind her, she glanced back to Andrei. "Let me know if you see anything."

He nodded and shouldered the gun. "Don't take too long."

Mercy nodded and turned to the first pool of blood. She had to approach it slowly due to all the crows around it. The birds were not in the least bit scared of her and that comfort near humans alarmed Mercy. She had to nudge them aside with her feet and they only skittered a few steps away. By the time she reached the bloody pool, she realized it was a grotesque watering hole. She squatted down carefully and filled a vial to the brim. Wiping the glass down with a spare cloth, she pocketed it.

The blood pool wasn't deep and only a few feet

wide, but as she got to her feet, her eyes drew up to an open doorway ahead of her.

It looked like the building was a grocer's store, but the shutters on the windows were all open. One of them hung by a single hinge, swinging in the morning breeze. Something was on the floor in the doorway. She couldn't quite make out what it was and drew closer to it.

Taking a few careful steps, Mercy navigated her way around the crows. Even more flew down to join the already enormous flock. The closer she got to the front door of the grocer's store, the fewer crows crowded around her feet, which made it easier to move. She took a deep breath, then stood in the decimated doorway.

Movement on the floor caught the light from outside. Something large lay between the countertop and a display that once held baskets of lettuce. Green leaves of lettuce littered the floor like confetti.

Mercy held still. Her first instinct was that it could be a werewolf, but her logical mind pushed that impulse aside. It was daytime. No werewolf would be out here. Still, her mouth went dry as she squatted down to iden-tify it. She couldn't simply leave without knowing. That wasn't an option. Her eyes fell on a single glove closer to her feet.

What she recognized as a glove she soon realized was not empty. She could see the gore from the severed wrist and the bloody puddle it sat in. Her eyes reluc-tantly shifted to the large moving mass closer to the vegetable display.

Her eyes adjusted to the light, and she realized the movement came from an enormous number of crows.

They had covered something, and their wings caught the light from the doorway as they climbed over each other in a grotesque feeding frenzy.

Mercy gasped.

One bird looked up at her sound and flew over to her. She jerked back, but it landed and picked at the gloved hand at her feet. It shifted the hand clumsily in its black beak before flying off behind her.

Her legs shaky, she stood up and turned around. That wasn't at all what she expected to find here. Then again, this was what happened after werewolves attacked. The crows were simply taking advantage of the food. Perhaps that was why there were so many of them in these woods.

Mercy got to the doorway, intending to go back to the Tortoise, back to Andrei where it was safe. A flash of metal across the street from one of the other decimated buildings drew her attention.

"Get back!" Andrei yelled. "Hurry and get back now! They're armed!"

Instead of running, Mercy's instincts kicked in. She backed into the shadows of the building then dropped to the ground. Gunfire shattered wood over her shoulder, sounding like thunder in the small, dark space. The loud noise startled the swarm.

In a mass of black wings and beaks, the birds shot past her. Their feathers brushed her skin. Their caws exploded the air as they flew by her ears. She felt the scratch of their claws as they emerged from the store. Mercy expected them to flee, to fly toward the trees for safety like normal birds. But they didn't. The man across the street tried to pull the wooden shutters closed in time, but the boards had been weakened from the werewolf attack and couldn't latch properly. The panicked birds flew straight toward him.

Mercy spotted the angry pale face and wide eyes of a squat man with brown hair just as he screamed. He wore a green housecoat that caught the sunlight, maybe silk or satin. The birds flew into the room with him, forcing him away from the window.

"Damn crows!" he cried, ducking as two birds flew past his head. "Out of my way! I have to stop that thief from defiling my brother!"

Mercy couldn't believe her ears. He thought she was a grave robber? After surviving a werewolf attack this gruesome, that's what he was afraid of?

She prepared herself to run while the birds kept the shooter distracted, but that gnawing curiosity took hold of her. Mercy needed to see. It was a ridiculous compulsion, and she knew it. She shouldn't look, but she also knew she would regret not looking back.

With the birds gone, she could see the blood trail where the hand had been torn from the body. It splattered across the floor and along the wall. The writhing mass she had seen when she first walked into the room was now bare and exposed save for a few remaining flailing crows that hadn't been spooked off. What she saw in their wake was the disemboweled body of a man whose upper and lower halves had been almost completely pulled in two.

Her heart beat faster in her chest.

In the morning light that spilled in from the open

door, she saw long claw marks along the legs and teeth marks around the remaining skin of the belly.

Stomach clenching, she finally looked away.

She knew what had made those marks. She recognized them from the deputy sheriff's body when she came upon Henry eating him that night ages ago. More than one werewolf had attacked him. At least two to pull him apart like that. But how many had fallen on Crowsmirth that night? Surely more than two to cause so much destruction.

A gunshot pulled her from her thoughts. She turned back to the door, shaking from head to toe, knowing she couldn't take cover forever.

"Come on!" Andrei called. The urgency in his voice made her move.

She got to her feet. Pumping her legs as hard as she could, she ran out of the shop. Across the street, the man was still struggling with the birds that had flown inside. He had tossed one awkwardly out the window, its wings flapping in panic and confusion. At least the gunman was distracted.

Most of the birds had fled the puddles when the gunshot went off, leaving her a clear path to the Tortoise. Andrei watched her with wide eyes, his rifle at the ready.

Mercy leaped over a wide puddle, listening to the whooshing of a flock of crows overhead and watching their shadows flicker and weave across the dirt road.

Another gunshot went off from behind her. She jumped, fighting the urge to drop down on the ground again.

"Come back here, thief!" the man cried.

Andrei took aim and shot. Wood splintered behind her. This time she didn't jump, she only focused on reaching the vehicle.

She dove in through the window. Andrei shifted the gun to one hand in a fluid, practiced motion before hitting the accelerator hard. One hand gripped the steering wheel and the other stayed on his gun.

Mercy pulled one leg into the seat and then the other, listening to the wild ramblings of the man screaming incoherent words behind them. His voice grew fainter as they drove past the main street of Crowsmirth and deeper into the woods.

They drove in silence for several minutes. Mercy took deep breaths to stop from shaking. Andrei kept glancing over at her, waiting for her to speak, but Mercy was trying to get her heart to stop racing.

"What was that all about?" Andrei cried, his voice filled with panic. "Why was that guy trying to shoot you?"

His knuckles blanched as he clung tight to the steering wheel and his other hand shook, still holding the heavy rifle. She gestured for the gun and he blinked as though he had forgotten he was still holding it. Mindful of the hot barrel, Mercy took it and then took his hand. His palm was sweaty as he squeezed her hand tight.

"Werewolves," she muttered, still trying to calm her nerves.

He glanced at her, squeezed her hand again. "Take your time. I want to hear what happened."

She told him what she had seen, even describing the bite marks on the body, the disemboweled corpse, and how the body had been nearly pulled in two. It clearly upset him to hear, but he needed to know. Andrei was used to being among werewolves, not witnessing their carnage.

"How did they break in? Like clearly that crazy man had a gun. That Liquid Lead compound is just down the street."

"Thomas isn't making it as much, remember? He's only taking live, unspoiled werewolves now so we can cure them."

Andrei shook his head. "Yeah, but what's the point of all those werewolf hunters if they can't trap any werewolves?"

Mercy considered that Thomas had said something similar. She let go of Andrei's hand so he could negotiate the winding, bumpy road. She remembered the large influx of werewolves that had been brought in to the mill the other day. Supposedly they were from a large capture organized by many werewolf hunters in Crowsmirth. If that was the case, why did the town get ravaged by more werewolves afterwards? Were the hunters not as successful as they seemed or were there simply that many werewolves in these woods? Was Crowsmirth taking the brunt of werewolf attacks and Kanta was next on the menu?

In Kanta, Thomas told her many hunters had never brought a single werewolf in to his mill. Their interest was in the flesh trade, not truly in werewolves like they pretended. If there were enough hunters in Crowsmirth to take down twenty werewolves in a single night, then where the hell were they?

"We may be dealing with a huge pack," she said. "The last grouping they brought to Thomas was around twenty, and that didn't include the ones that Thomas didn't have room for. Even after a capture like there, there are still enough here to bring Crowsmirth to its knees. They probably let their guard down, thinking the biggest threat was over, but there are still a lot more in these woods."

She glanced at the rearview mirror and saw the big flock of crows flying over the town in the distance. "I think we can exclude that guy back there as a hunter."

Andrei scoffed as drove onto a rickety wooden bridge. "Yeah, that guy was crazy. If he was a hunter, then he was a terrible shot. I don't know what's worse, getting bitten by a werewolf, or losing your mind if you survive an attack."

The creek moved slowly but steadily beneath them as Andrei maneuvered the Tortoise over the sun-bleached pine boards of a bridge that had clearly seen better days.

"We should be close to the camp," Mercy said as the vehicle dropped back onto the rocky dirt path on the opposite side of the bridge. "Thomas said they weren't far from the water."

Andrei nodded and pulled the Tortoise into the underbrush and off the main road. Tree branches snapped as the vehicle dipped into a ditch. It was made for uneven terrain and wooded places, Thomas had told them. It was time to find out if he was right.

"Let's go deeper," she said.

Andrei glanced at her, concern in his eyes. Neither of them wanted to be stuck out here for good.

"I know, but we're still sitting ducks this close to the road. This thing is fully decked out, but it's going to draw attention if it can be seen from the road." She patted the metal door affectionately. "I have a feeling they would know Thomas built it too. It's got his bizarre signature all over it. I would rather nobody know we're here."

With a deep sigh, Andrei nodded. "Okay, let's see what this baby can do."

He switched gears and revved the Tortoise up out of the ditch and deeper into the woods, careful not to run into the massive pine trees along the way.

THE SCENT OF GRASS, decaying leaves, and steam exhaust overwhelmed Mercy as she stepped out of the vehicle. Andrei had found a tiny clearing to park the Tortoise, one that would be defensible if they had to go that route.

They wanted to have space to put up the electric shields and not burn the whole forest to the ground. Given how old and thick the forest was, that was definitely a possibility if they weren't careful.

Mercy grabbed her pistol and secured it in her hip holster. She grabbed two satchels of needles and secured them to her thighs. Both were made with leather and drawstring closures so they couldn't fall out if they ran into trouble.

After their experience in Crowsmirth earlier, Mercy didn't want to take any chances. Her final step was pulling on the wolf helmet created by Thomas. She pulled off the wrappings, grateful for the breeze on her face, and pocketed the fabric. The helmet rested lightly on her shoulders and fit perfectly over her head. She dropped the green visor down and looked for the position of the sun. It was directly overhead.

So much for the early head start they had made. If she hadn't insisted on them stopping at Crowsmirth, they could have already found the camp by now. Mercy could only blame herself. Andrei had certainly not wanted to stay. She had been the one eager to investigate.

She sighed. Pulling open the back door, she reached into the basket on the back seat and pulled out their waterskins and trail mix. They could have a very long day ahead of them. After closing the door, she went around the back to check on Andrei.

"Here. We need to eat." She held up his waterskin and a bar of oats.

Andrei held his wolf helmet in his hands, shaking his head. "Doesn't this seem a little much to you?"

She smiled. "What? You don't like it? I think it's great! It's going to be a perfect distraction if we need it."

He grabbed his waterskin and bundle of trail mix, eating a handful before continuing. "Or a target. I don't need a helmet to say I'm a wolf. I'm already one. It feels fake."

She took a long drink from her waterskin and rubbed his shoulder. "It's meant to make them only remember these helmets instead of what we look like. You don't want them to know who you are, or that you're an actual werewolf."

He sighed, turning the mask over in his hands. "You're right, I guess. I don't know. It feels weird to me."

She reached over, unraveled his face wrappings, and put them into his hand. Then she leaned in close and pecked a kiss on his cheek.

Andrei blinked, his eyes wide.

"It's not for the werewolves, it's for the hunters," she reminded him. "It keeps you from being identified and hunted down later. Thomas is right, if they ever find out we're responsible for curing werewolves, they will come after us. We are a direct threat to their way of life."

He nodded and glanced away from her. She pocketed her own food and drink then reached over to take the helmet from him. It was lightweight in her hands as she reached up to fit the mask over his head.

He moved his head around, adjusting to it. "When you put it like that, maybe it's not too bad after all."

She rubbed his shoulder. "Exactly. Anything to keep our faces out of the limelight." She leaned in close and pecked a kiss on the back of his neck. His skin was warm against her lips.

He lifted his shoulders and put an arm around her waist. "Yes, ma'am," he said. "Whatever you say, ma'am."

She giggled and playfully pushed him away, rolling her eyes dramatically. "Whatever."

THANK goodness she had a good head for direction, Mercy thought to herself. They had been wandering around in the woods for hours, looking for any sign of the werewolf pack they knew had to live out here. They had followed Thomas's vague orders and ventured out past the creek. For some reason Mercy expected them to be just a few feet away, but she knew better than that, didn't she? Werewolves were never easy to find.

Andrei thought he could catch their scent, but the deeper they went into the forest, the less confident he seemed to be. Mercy knew she could find her way back to the Tortoise if they had to resort to that, but she hoped that didn't happen. She didn't like the idea of having to pass back through Crowsmirth. It was too dangerous, and the idea of coming out here day after day made her nervous. But as the sun continued its march across the sky, she almost resigned herself to that reality.

"We'll need to head back soon and try again later," she said, trailing behind Andrei as he led the way, sniffing the air as they went.

Andrei didn't respond. Ever since she asked him to see if he could track their target, he seemed to take the responsibility seriously. It was like he was trying to prove himself to her, as if he hadn't already done that a hundred times over. While she appreciated his determination, she was getting worried. She didn't want to be stuck in these woods after dark. Her mind kept flickering back to the body of the grocer covered in crows and the two werewolves that had tried to pull the man in two.

"Andrei?" she asked.

He didn't turn around and even started walking faster. Mercy had to pump her legs to keep up with him.

"Andrei, did you hear me?" She touched his arm and he jumped. She pulled back, completely surprised.

His eyes had gone wide and his pupils were dilated. He had crouched forward in a stiff, angular pose that reminded her of when he transformed. She had watched him often enough to know it well. It was disturbing to see him with it during the light of day and still completely human.

Andrei blinked a few times before his eyes returned to normal. He pushed his helmet back and rubbed at his eyes. "Sorry, I forgot you were there… I forgot where I was, I think."

She took his hand. "If this is getting to you, maybe we should go back."

"No, it's okay." He gave an apologetic smile. "I guess I just got too involved. I caught something up ahead. It's faint, but it definitely smells like werewolf."

Mercy beamed. "Their camp?"

"Maybe."

"Let's go then!"

Andrei led the way as they pushed through the underbrush. He walked so quickly that Mercy had to do a light run to keep up. Above their heads a flock of crows flew through the sky, filling their air with their caws. Mercy kept glancing up at them. She remembered the brush of their feathers against her skin as they flew out of the grocer's shop. It was so strange how they went for the man with the gun instead of to the sky like most birds would. The birds here didn't act like normal birds.

She pushed down the urge to ask Andrei to slow down even as she panted. Instead, she swallowed down the urge and ran close behind him.

She expected to see a clearing emerge out of the woods, similar to what the pack at Kanta had. She didn't expect a partially dilapidated wooden fence surrounding a ravaged home.

6

CAGED

THE DRY WOOD CRACKED beneath her fingers as Mercy gripped the squared off beam of the fence. Weakened by too many warm summers and harsh winters, pieces of the wood fell off at her touch. Her father had built a similar one around their home, meant to be a barricade to hold off werewolves, with tin cans and metal car parts laced through in haphazard patterns, but that was where the similarities ended. Unlike her father's fence, this was not built well. It wouldn't keep a rabbit out, let alone a werewolf.

Andrei crouched down, looking closer at a portion of the gate that had been torn to pieces. Long claw marks went down the cross beams of the wood. Carefully constructed metal had been torn asunder. Wooden scraps and metal pieces lay on the ground beneath the weak point, a small reminder of the destruction that took place there. Judging by the state of the fence, this damage wasn't recent.

"Is this where they are?" Mercy asked. Her gaze

went to the looming house beyond the trees. It was hard to tell from this distance, but she could just spot enormous holes that pocketed the sides of the building. It could have been reflections from some metal sheeting, but she doubted it. The holes didn't catch the light. They reminded her of gaping wounds. Honestly, she was surprised the place was still standing.

Andrei put his nose close to the gashes in the fence and closed his eyes. "No, this is old. Maybe a couple of weeks, possibly more, I think. This was opened up a while ago."

"So we're at the wrong place?"

He shook his head. "I don't know about that. Werewolves have definitely been here recently. The whole space smells of them, but the wreckage here is not recent."

Mercy's gaze was pulled back toward the house. "So they travel through here."

Andrei climbed back to his feet, stretching his legs. "I'd say regularly. Maybe they've holed up here in order to have a roof over their head. If we had cover like this back at camp, we would have commandeered it in an instant," he added with a short laugh. "This place might look run down to you, but to us it would've been a gift. No getting rained on, no freezing wind, and there might even be some supplies."

He saw the good in this lost land, but the whole place felt off to her. Mercy couldn't put her finger on it, but something was wrong, and she had a nagging feeling that werewolves didn't live here. She hadn't spotted any blood puddles like she had around the camp in Kanta, and if she was a werewolf, this would have been a healthy distance from the building for a nightly transformation. But she trusted Andrei's senses. If the local werewolves came through here often, then there could be clues to their whereabouts. Even if they weren't camping out here, it was still a clue.

"Let's keep an eye out for footprints or anything else we could use to track them," she said, stepping over the fence, cautious of the splinters and rubble beneath it.

Andrei nodded and followed her. Together they headed down the dirt path that led to the house. At one point, this had likely been a sort of driveway to the house. She could sort of make out where the wheel tracks used to be, but now the weeds and grass had overgrown everything, making it a loose path at best. A couple of weeks or more since the werewolves got in, Andrei had told her. These weeds had been spreading for longer than a few measly weeks. More like at least a month.

As they walked, Mercy noted the thick grass and weeds growing on either side of the path. They would have come up to her knees if they were walking through that. From the looks of this place, nobody other than werewolves had been here in a long time. So why were the werewolves coming here?

"Over there!" Andrei hurried over to a spot near the tall weeds. He crouched down to a patch of empty dirt, one of the few remaining on the path. A pair of werewolf paw prints were visible. One had been clipped by the weeds. "So they were transformed when they came here. They were heading toward the building."

Mercy crouched down beside them, her mind going back to the training her father had given her years ago. "The weight is on the toes, not the full foot. They're not strolling in, they're running toward the house." She pointed out another pair to the side on another patch of dirt.

Andrei stepped out of the way so his shadow wouldn't obscure her work.

"Two more over there. See how they're toe heavy? That means they're running."

He nodded slowly before glancing back up to the house. "Maybe this is part of their hunting range."

"That's not comforting."

Andrei gave a nervous laugh. "It's daytime, so they won't be transformed now." He shrugged. "But transformed werewolves don't run back home, so this isn't their camp."

They got to their feet in silence. Mercy wanted to remind him it wouldn't be daytime forever. If she had stumbled across a place like this with her father, they never would have pressed on, but she had very different goals now. Her father wouldn't have dared go through the gate. The thought made her proud. "Let's keep going. We should find out what they're running toward."

Andrei hissed a breath, "Hopefully not toward more corpses like back in Crowsmirth."

"Corpses wouldn't last for weeks," she reminded him. "It's got to be something else."

The remains of an orchard littered the grounds around the home. Despite the state of the building, the trees were well tended. The squat trunks and wide branches were covered in new green leaves, and the farther they walked in, the more trees they could see. Each tree was evenly spaced from the next.

"Two acres, easy, for the orchard. At least what we can see. Maybe there's more," Mercy said when they took a bend in the path. "The gate is a mess but the trees are well cared for. Somebody is tending to them."

"All the werewolves are running in for free fruit. That's got to be it." Andrei laughed.

Mercy rolled her eyes but couldn't suppress a smile despite her nerves. Her gaze shifted back to the house looming over the acres of land like a silent observer. At one point it was probably a beautiful building. Light blue paint was still visible on the parts of the house that hadn't had holes torn through the walls. Someone had once cared deeply about this place. On the side closest to the path, however, a great gaping maw beckoned to them. Another one was visible near the front too, as though something bad had happened to the foundation. The place would have surely collapsed with such destructive damage, but the bones were solid, so the home remained. It would succumb to its fate at some point, but for now it stood against the elements against all expectations.

Somewhere in the empty blackness of that maw Mercy noted movement out of the corner of her eye. But when she looked directly, she saw nothing. She had been taught to pay attention to her instincts though, and the hairs on the back of her neck stood up. She put a hand out to Andrei's arm, bringing them both to a halt.

Her gaze looked for any other movement, any other sign of life again, but it was gone.

"What is it?" Andrei asked.

"I just… I thought I saw movement."

His shoulders tensed as he stared at the building. "Where? The house?"

"Inside that hole close to the path. It could have been a trick of the light, I guess," she added, second guessing herself.

He took her hand. "Don't do that. Trust your instincts. It can't hurt to be too cautious. For all the evidence we've seen of werewolves around here, I haven't seen any of them. It makes me nervous. Here, let me take the lead."

Mercy let him. She found it cute that he was being protective of her. All the same, she unsnapped her holster but didn't take the pistol out. Not yet, at least. She didn't want to accidentally shoot Andrei. Sure, the silver might not hurt him like it used to, but it was still a bullet. She didn't want to take any chances.

Tensing his arms at his sides, Andrei shifted his hands and forearms. Black claws erupted through his fingertips and coarse fur trailed down his arm to his elbow. A trickle of blood dripped down to his feet. Andrei flexed his new hands and fingers as though limbering them up. Even though Mercy had seen him a hundred times as a werewolf, he was far more menacing as a human with clawed hands and arms at his sides.

"Is that a good idea?" she asked.

"What?" He glanced back to her with a smirk. "I've got to protect us!"

"Yeah, but aren't you afraid we'll spook them?"

He looked at his hands. "I mean, I'm not a full were-wolf here. That's not as scary, right?"

Mercy was looking at Andrei, but her gaze was pulled by more movement from the house behind him. Something was coming toward them, some kind of swarm was erupting from the broken gash in the house. She couldn't focus on what it was.

Andrei looked toward the house then shouted, "Get down!"

Mercy did as he said, dropping to the dirt in an instant. Andrei crouched down with her, putting his arms around her. She could still see the house beneath his arm and watch the shadow fill the sky. She could hear them now. It was a cacophony of flapping wings.

Crows. Just like at Crowsmirth. Only this time there were far more.

They filled the sky, briefly hiding the clouds and sun before dispersing into disarray. Instead of flying away like normal birds, they flew to the orchard. There they landed, cawing and watching Mercy and Andrei, as though weighing whether they should attack them.

"It's only birds," Andrei said standing up, relief in his voice.

Only birds. He said that like the ones in Crowsmirth hadn't flown right into a gunman's face. Mercy couldn't relax. She thought of the crows feasting on the grocer just hours before and drinking from puddles of blood. Growing up in the woods, she was certainly no expert on wildlife, but she had run off into the forest whenever she could during the day. She had never seen birds act like this before. It was uncanny.

Andrei got to his feet, transforming his hands back to normal. He was getting faster at it, and cleaner too. He put a hand out to help her up. "I guess that solves the mystery of what the werewolves come here for: easy prey."

Mercy let him help her to her feet. She wished she could feel as comfortable with that explanation, but it didn't make sense. Werewolves didn't go after birds, not that she had heard at least. They went for humans. Their curse, or rather the venom of their infection, forced them to crave killing humans more than animals.

She dusted off her knees, turning to look around at all the crows. Some were preening with one wing in the air, others nuzzled, but most had their eyes on them. She wasn't mistaken. The birds had surrounded them. That wasn't normal for any wild animal behavior as far as she could recall. Then again, had she ever paid attention to crow behavior? She had heard them growing up, but rarely seen them in flocks. They were usually a backdrop to the more important matters in her life. Maybe this was all perfectly normal behavior, and she simply hadn't noticed it before.

"You shouldn't be here," a high-pitched voice said.

Mercy snapped her head back toward the house. A girl with dark eyes and matching black hair, her pale skin grungy with dirt stood on the path. She looked around their age, possibly younger, and wore a frayed black dress with a pair of muddied black boots. In her right hand she held a pistol not too different from Mercy's own. It was aimed at them.

"Trespassers are to be shot on sight." The girl cocked the gun with far more comfort than Mercy ever had. Around them the crows fluttered their wings and hopped between branches. They all started cawing at them. It was as if the birds were part of a show and Mercy and Andrei were the unwilling performers.

"Wait," Andrei said, clearly just as shocked as Mercy. "You're human?"

Mercy glanced at him in confusion. Why was that the first question he asked? Then she realized what he meant. How in the world could a human exist out here in the middle of nowhere with werewolves running here probably every night? That one pistol wasn't enough to keep a whole pack at bay.

Before the girl could say anything, Mercy asked, "How in the world have you survived out here? Are you alone?"

The girl smirked. "Is that so hard to believe? My pets here are an excellent warning system."

"I see…" Andrei moved closer to Mercy.

"We're not trespassers," Mercy clarified. "I mean, not intentionally anyway. We're looking for the werewolf camp around here. We didn't expect to find… anyone else."

The girl frowned. "You're not dressed like hunters, that's for sure. I've never seen any of them wear ridiculous helmets like those."

Andrei glanced at Mercy with a look in his eye like he was holding back an *I told you so.*

"What do you want with a werewolf pack, anyway?" The girl asked.

"It's complicated," Mercy admitted, not knowing where to even start.

"Maybe it would be easier to talk if you weren't trying to shoot us." Andrei put an arm around Mercy's waist as though he was ready to toss her into his arms and speed back toward the fence if needed.

The girl huffed in annoyance before holstering the gun. "No, I guess not. But if you try anything, know that my birds have a taste for eyes." She pointed a finger at her own eye with a laugh.

Despite her threats, but Mercy relaxed. The crows were one thing, and the loaded gun another. But Mercy didn't take her words to be an empty threat. Looking around at the many birds that roosted in the trees, she could easily see them attacking an unwanted trespasser. Especially if they were a hunter. Hunters usually dressed light and had weapons for bigger prey than birds. Guns wouldn't stop a flock of birds.

The fact that this girl had trained them to attack was alarming.

Mercy looked at her again, trying to understand her. Beneath the bravado and threats, she looked undernourished. Now that Mercy thought about it, the gun might not even be loaded, but that didn't mean she wasn't dangerous. It took skill to survive in the middle of the woods without even a barricade to keep safe. That kind of ability wasn't something to take lightly. While the scare tactics probably kept most from messing with her, it also meant she didn't do trades for supplies. She was probably living under a time limit before a resource ran out.

"Crowsmirth has been completely overrun by werewolves," Mercy stated, quietly glad to see the disappointment in the girl's eyes. "And the only people left alive there look to be mad. Were any of them relations of yours?"

"No," she said, her voice small as a sad resignation came across her face. "No, my parents got eaten months ago."

"By werewolves?" Andrei asked. Good, he was picking up the pieces too and possibly coming to the same conclusions.

The girl nodded.

"I'm sorry to hear that," Mercy shifted her weight and nodded to the house behind her. "So you live alone."

The girl's eyes flickered first to fear then anger as her hand went for the gun again. "That's none of your business!"

Mercy reached up and pulled off her wolf helmet allowing the girl to see who she really was—a person, not a faceless enemy.

"Don't—!" Andrei cried, but she ignored him.

Mercy put the helmet under her arm and walked up to her. The girl was holding the gun out again, but her hands were shaking and her eyes were wide. It took her a moment to speak. Mercy stared at her and the barrel hoping that her gamble had paid off.

"You're… like me," the girl said, dropping her hand to the side and lowering the gun.

"I am." Mercy took a deep breath to calm her nerves. In that instant, she saw herself in the girl's eyes: frightened but determined, lost but brave, in a losing situation but unable to fully see it. Not yet anyway. If things had been a little different for Mercy, a trap not set right or the barrier not kept going one evening, she might have even been in the same situation.

Mercy put a hand on the girl's shoulder, realizing how frail she felt under her grip. She was shaking. "It's hard living on your own, isn't it?"

Tears sprung to her eyes, but she didn't respond.

Mercy softened her voice, worried it might crack with the weight of her words. "It's even harder being a girl in this world."

She blinked and licked her dry lips. "They tried to capture me when I went into town on my own," she admitted, taking a breath. "I didn't even know who they were! They chased me." A tear slid down her cheek and Mercy nodded.

"I know. They're monsters, aren't they?"

She didn't respond, only stared as if reliving the nightmare again in her head. "I ran. My birds attacked them. I kept going. I ran until I threw up. Then I ran some more until I got home." She looked up at the trees, her eyes wide and pained. "My friends… they saved my life. They led me home. They brought me back to safety. If I hadn't had them…"

Mercy rubbed her back, expecting her to cry, but the girl wiped at her eyes. She took a shaky breath and swallowed down the tears.

"I'm Kit," she said, extending a hand.

Mercy took her hand. "I'm Mercy, and this is Andrei."

Andrei stepped up beside them, removing his own helmet, and shook Kit's hand as well. "We're together," he said, with a nod toward Mercy.

Mercy stared at him with wide eyes. Since when did he start making announcements? "Can you be a little less awkward?"

"What?" He shrugged with a grin. "It's true!"

Kit gave a short laugh and wiped at her eyes again.

Mercy took a deep breath before broaching the tough question. "I know this may seem like a weird question but..." Mercy swallowed. "Would you like to come live with us?"

"Me?" Kit asked, looking between the two of them.

"Yeah, why not?" Andrei gave her a smile. "It's got to be better than this." He gestured to the house behind her that looked like it was decaying in place.

Kit looked at Mercy for a long moment then turned to Andrei. "I almost shot you!"

Andrei barked a laugh. "Yeah, that happens. It's kind of a thing with us."

"Kit, you can't stay here. You're drawing werewolves here all the time. We can tell by their tracks. I don't know how you've been avoiding them, but—"

"I hide," Kit said, as though in a rush to get the words out. "I hide in the cage."

"The... cage?" Andrei asked, glancing at Mercy with concern.

Mercy pursed her lips. She knew they were both

thinking the same thing: did they really want to see the cage?

———

AS RUN DOWN and inhospitable as the house looked from the outside, it looked even worse inside. Almost all the exposed wood was covered in claw marks, from the walls to the furniture. The floor was covered by a blanket of debris and it smelled of rotten leaves and bird droppings. Walking through the place was difficult and Mercy grappled to keep her balance just to keep up. The nest in the old chandelier that swung far above their heads proved that the crows roosted here, living here in the empty shell of the home.

Kit bounded over the piles of debris and rotten leaves with ease, dodging around shattered furniture and avoiding the occasional spiderweb. "This used to be the living room, but it's kind of become my home now. The stairs fell down a month ago, but that's not a big deal 'cause I don't really need anything upstairs anymore."

The stairs, or rather the pile of debris that sat where they used to stand, had turned into splintered lumber and dangerous metal spikes that jutted out of the ground. It was easy to imagine Kit hurting herself on them. All it would take was falling and she could get killed, with nobody knowing any better. With the werewolves out here, a severe wound would be enough to be lethal come nightfall.

"I guess the house got too unstable?" Andrei asked,

eyes reflecting Mercy's concern as he surveyed the damage.

Kit shook her head as she traipsed into the kitchen and picked up a loaf of bread that had clearly been stolen. "No, there were too many werewolves on them. They're way bigger in person, so I think with about ten of them on the stairs at once, it was just too much. The whole house shook when they fell! I was afraid the place was going to collapse when it happened. But this place is pretty sturdy."

Mercy narrowed her eyes. "Ten werewolves? That many come here?" She looked at the damage with a new perspective. The clawed up walls, the destruction of the stairs, the floor that wasn't even visible beneath it all. Then she spotted it. Around the corner in the kitchen stood a large cage that barely fit in the room. She recognized it immediately.

"It's a werewolf cage," she whispered in awe. "That's where you go? You stay in the cage overnight?"

"Yep! Here, let me show you." She put the loaf of bread aside and moved around the piles of debris. When she stepped inside the cage, the door squealed on its hinges as she pulled it closed with a metal slam. "I step inside and lock myself in, like so."

She picked up a piece of wood and jammed it into the lock.

"And done! Safe and sound for the night!"

Andrei went over and shook the cage door. The wooden makeshift lock rattled against the metal. "So… what you're telling us is that this flimsy piece of wood is all that stands between you and an army of hungry, transformed werewolves?"

Kit's grin faded. "It's lasted me for three months. It isn't that flimsy."

"More like you've just been lucky," he insisted, and shoved a few more times against the cage door until the wooden dowel fell to the ground with a clatter. The cage door swung an inch open. Kit's mouth hung open as she stared at it. "If I can do this so easily, so can they. And if there are so many they can topple a staircase? You won't be lucky for much longer, Kit."

Mercy stepped closer to the cage, her arms folded in front of her, as Kit stepped out. "Do you know where the werewolves are coming from? It has to be farther in, away from Crowsmirth."

Kit gave a sarcastic laugh. "I still can't believe you're really looking for them."

"We are." Mercy kept her gaze steady as Kit gazed at her with a mixture of shock and horror.

"Are you crazy?" she asked.

Mercy gave a heavy sigh. "No, we want to help them."

"Help them?" Kit scrunched up her face, one hand hovering against the cage door as if she would close herself inside again. "You mean kill them."

Mercy was about to explain, but Andrei interrupted.

"Would you like that, Kit?" He licked his lips. "It's got to be tough being inches from their claws every night. I can't imagine what it was like watching them kill your parents." Andrei studied her, looking for some sign, but Mercy didn't know what. Was he testing her?

Confirming that she wouldn't try to kill the werewolves once they found them?

Kit bit her lips and looked between them. Normally folks had immediate opinions about what they thought of werewolves, or especially what to do with them, so her hesitance was strange.

"I don't want them dead," she finally blurted.

"You don't?" Andrei feigned surprise and slight disgust. "Why the hell not? They would kill you in a heartbeat. I know you know that."

She gave a nervous nod, avoided his gaze, and started fidgeting her fingers together. "They… saved me the first night they came and knocked down the fencing. Pa had forgotten to refill the steam engine with coal that day and the fire went out. The fence was supposed to be electrified but fell apart like paper to the werewolves." She paused, breathing hard, and Mercy knew in that moment that she had told no one about this before. Three months, she had said before, was that when this happened? Of course, who was there to tell besides the crows?

Both Mercy and Andrei stayed silent, allowing Kit to gather herself together before she continued.

"They weren't really my ma and pa," she stated with her head lowered and fingers tied up in knots. "They bought me when I was five. My real mom was captured just like I was, at our home. Once Ma and Pa bought me, I never saw my real mom again."

A tear streaked down Kit's cheek, but she didn't wipe it away.

"My new folks wanted help around the farm. They

wanted free labor. I cried a lot at first, but Pa grabbed a switch from one of the peach trees and I learned to *appreciate* my new parents. I learned to *appreciate* my new life and chores, but I never ever forgot who I really was. To keep from getting hurt, I pretended they were my parents, just like I pretended my name was Katherine—but that wasn't really me. I had to be Katherine to survive. But I'm Kit." She shook her head. "I know it's wrong, but I was so happy when I realized the were-wolves had killed them."

Andrei ran a hand through his hair, "Damn, Kit."

"Pa ran out to check the steam engine and Ma told me to grab a gun, but I didn't." A crazed smile crawled across Kit's face. "Instead I climbed in the werewolf cage—the same one Ma used to lock me in when I cried or complained—and I cried tears of absolute joy as those werewolves tore them apart."

Her cheeks wet with tears, Kit shook from head to toe. Mercy went to her, held her shoulders and stared into her eyes. "Don't feel guilty for that. They hurt you, tried to brainwash you, and you fought back. You didn't have a choice."

Kit nodded, no longer able to speak, and wrapped her arms around Mercy in a tight, desperate hug. Mercy held her close, let her cry, let her release all the pent up fear and pain and guilt that filled her. She glanced to Andrei who had a hand to his mouth. His eyes were glassy as he stared at them both. He gave her an appre-ciative nod, and she smiled back at him. At the camp in Kanta, Mercy wasn't sure if she could have empathy like Andrei could. Yet here she was flinging herself at this girl and taking her under her wing. But Mercy knew why. Kit's story resonated with her. It was like they were sisters. So Mercy wanted to protect her from anything she could.

Mercy cleared her throat before she spoke. "Sounds like they wanted you to forget who you were, so they could mold you into who they wanted you to be."

Pulling away, Kit's breath hitched in her throat. "So you don't think I'm a monster?"

"Clearly they were the monsters," Mercy said, and her heart filled with rage at the thought. If this had happened to Kit, how many other women and children were in a similar trap? Did all roads really lead back to the sick human traffickers who first tried to kidnap Mercy?

As Kit dried her eyes and Andrei helped her pack up her few belongings, Mercy knew just how close she came to being stuck in a similar cage.

7

LOSING DAYLIGHT

EVERYTHING KIT OWNED and wanted to bring with her could fit into a pair of leather satchels. Really, the few good items probably could have fit into one, but Mercy didn't want to ask that of her. Kit had lost enough. She couldn't bring herself to make her leave even more behind.

The clothes Kit packed were full of holes. At Mercy's insistence, she had pulled on a pair of leather pants that were probably the most undamaged piece of clothing she had. She pulled on a loose tunic and Mercy tied it at the waist. She had an extra pair of shoes that were held together by a few threads and put one in each of the satchels. Everything was practical, nothing looked personal or sentimental. After barely filling half of each satchel, she finally split the stale loaf of bread in half and stuffed the pieces on top.

Mercy wanted to say something, to tell her they had plenty of bread back at the mill, so she didn't need to worry about a stale loaf of bread. She wanted to tell her they had granola mix in the Tortoise and she didn't need to bring additional food. But she held her tongue. If bringing it made Kit feel better, made her feel prepared, she needed as much of that security as she could get. She had survived horrors Mercy could only imagine.

Glancing over at the cage again, Mercy noticed how small it was. Kit was lucky the cage sat against the wall. Then again, give the werewolves long enough and they would have found a way through that barrier. She had seen how voracious they could be when near a human. They would hurt themselves just to get a single bite. Mercy glanced around to the opposite side of the kitchen wall and saw that her suspicions were true. The wall was visibly damaged, meaning they were often clawing through, trying to get at her door. That was probably why she had been safe for three months, but she wouldn't have lasted one week more. They hadn't quite made it through the wooden beams yet, but they would have. The remaining wall showed their fury. Mercy shivered.

The werewolves and Kit's abusive parents hadn't left much for her to keep for herself. No, they weren't her parents, Mercy reminded herself. They had purchased her. They bought her only to keep their land and to maintain their home. Now most of the house was destroyed, torn to shreds by the werewolves, and what little Kit owned before was even less now. Let her keep the bread if it helped her keep going. Plenty of work remained to be done, and they might need the additional food if things got bad enough. Perhaps Kit was more prepared for what lay ahead than they were.

Mercy flung the leather strap of one bag over her shoulder, wincing at how light it was compared to what she expected. Kit picked up the other bag. She looked around the house one last time, taking deep breaths as though she was trying to keep from crying.

"This is it," Mercy said. "Are you ready?"

Kit turned to her abruptly, as though remembering she was there. She smiled. "I think so."

"Come on. Andrei is keeping watch outside, and the night is creeping up on us."

Kit shivered, turned and looked at the house once more and then took a deep breath. Finally she nodded and followed.

Mindful of her steps, Mercy emerged out of the gaping hole in the house and gazed up at the sky. The sun had dipped farther than she liked and the light was taking on an orange hue. They didn't have much time left.

Andrei came over to join her. "No movement other than the crows. But it's getting late." He glanced to Kit and then back to Mercy, his eyes questioning.

"We're good to leave," Mercy said and saw him visibly relax. Together they turned to the path back to the broken fence.

"Good. We can either head for the camp and hope to help them while it's daylight, or we find a place to crash for the night and try again tomorrow." He glanced back into the house as though truly considering them staying there for the night.

Mercy shook her head. "No way. I'd rather drive back to the mill before we attempt anything like that. If

Crowsmirth was any indication, I don't think there's just one werewolf camp out here. There's probably several. If Kit got attacked here, but there were still plenty who went for the town too, that means there must be a bunch. The Tortoise gives some protection, so hopefully it'll last until we get back to Kanta."

Andrei rubbed at his chin. "So we drive through Crowsmirth again? At dusk? That guy shot at you. I don't know if it's a good idea to go back so soon. Those werewolves will be after that corpse you found at the very least. At least here there's a cage——"

"No," she said again and started down the path that weaved through the orchard. Andrei hurried to catch up. The crows stood sentry in the branches of the trees. Peach trees, Kit had told them. The many birds fluttered their wings and cawed at them as they passed. How many of them were there? Could Kit really talk to them?

Kit ran to catch up, her pistol shoved into the waist of her pants. She waved wordlessly to the birds as they walked, and the crows seemed to get excited. Mercy hoped they wouldn't follow. That really would put her on edge if they did.

Andrei kept glancing back to the house, as though he was actually considering it as a refuge still. Mercy had to resist the urge to take his arm and drag him away from that place. Maybe she should have shown him the damage to the wall. Regardless, he wasn't being rational. He was thinking with the desperation that served him at the campsite, but it wouldn't help him now. That place was a deathtrap. Just because it could stand against a pack of werewolves didn't make it any more safe or reliable. She refused to be trapped there. The idea of the three of them crowding into that single cage and expecting not get clawed up or bitten was ludicrous. But at Andrei's old camp, a place like this house could mean surviving a few more winters, a shelter against the heat and cold. She understood his perspective, but that didn't help them now.

"So you all don't know where to go next?" Kit asked, turning away from her birds. Thankfully none of them had flown into the air yet to follow, and Mercy hoped it stayed that way. "Do you know this area at all?"

Mercy shook her head.

"Downtown Crowsmirth was a disaster." Andrei sighed. "Other than heading back to the mill, I don't know where we should head next. But that's a long drive." He glanced toward Mercy as he said it. She knew it was a long drive. She wasn't going to change her mind and stay regardless of what he said. "I don't know if we'll make it through Crowsmirth in time to escape nightfall."

Kit grimaced. "They have an inn down there. I know 'cause my captors would go spend the weekend there when they wanted to spend some time by themselves. I never got to go, of course, but I know it's there."

Mercy smiled. It was good to hear her refer to them as her captors instead of as her parents. They weren't her parents. They had never been her parents.

Andrei shook his head and dragged his hands over his face. "You think we should get a room at an inn where werewolves have killed a bunch of people already, where there's a madman with a gun looking to kill us, and where there are who knows how many corpses that could draw another enormous werewolf attack. And somehow that's a better idea than staying here?"

Mercy narrowed her eyes at Andrei. "We are not staying here. I will not be killed in this death trap. It isn't safe. You proved that yourself. Now let it go."

Andrei sighed but gave a short, resigned nod.

Kit crossed her arms. "How long will it take to drive back to the mill in Kanta?"

Mercy glanced to the sun's position. Arguing only wasted their time, but they had to do something. "Two hours to drive, possibly longer if it gets dark, and half an hour to get to the car."

Kit nodded, glancing up to the sky. "That sun means we have a little over an hour to get someplace safe and, no offense, but my cage isn't big enough for all three of us to fit."

"Yeah, I know." Andrei sighed, clearly eager to change the subject. "What about the Tortoise? It's a modified vehicle," he explained to Kit. "Thomas put an electric fence around it to prevent any werewolves from getting in. That should keep them out."

Mercy winced but gave a reluctant nod. "That might work, but Thomas said it had a limit of about ten were-wolves. More than that and it could fail. Then the Tortoise becomes a death trap too."

Kit gave a nervous laugh. "There are definitely more than ten. There are hundreds."

Mercy and Andrei glanced at her.

"Hundreds?" Andrei asked, his eyes wide. "Are you sure?"

"Look, I had plenty of time to count them and I've seen them every night for the past few months. I didn't get the same ones every night." She glanced back to her old home that was slowly being hidden by the orchard as they walked. "My folks had an electric fence to keep them out too, and you see how effective that was against them. Three of them got fried to death, but the rest of them waltzed in like it was no big deal. An electric fence is not enough."

Andrei glanced to Mercy, his throat bobbing as he swallowed. Mercy agreed. This information completely changed things. If they had known what they were walking into here, they never would have come out to Crowsmirth on their own. They never would have chosen this place as their first stop outside of Kanta, or as a place to experiment with the Tortoise. This was far more dangerous than any of them knew, even Thomas.

It was bad enough imagining werewolves frying to death on an electric fence, but knowing the pack was that coordinated when they were in beast form was unsettling. She could almost picture them climbing over other bodies to get to the prey within. Could these were-wolves be different from the ones in Kanta? No, that wasn't possible. They were treated with her partial cure the same way the others were, so physically they weren't that different. Perhaps it was because of their sheer numbers, there was a greater chance one of them got inside, got wind of food, or threw themselves onto an active fence.

Mercy wanted to know so much, to understand and sort out all these clues, so she could better know what they were up against. But that simply wasn't possible. They had no time for curiosity or research. It was just like the corpse she saw at the grocery store earlier—there was no time to investigate, so his death was written off as a simple werewolf attack and forgotten. Another clue lost to limited time.

"Mercy?" Andrei asked, "you've gotten quiet." A small smile tugged at his cute lips and she had to force down the urge to kiss him. "Care to share with the class what's on your mind?"

"Sure, if you'll quit being smart about it."

He grinned. It was his superpower and he knew it, damn it.

"I think Kit is right. We head for the inn wearing disguises. I know they might recognize us from before, but we'll have to deal with that when we get there. These woods are going to be far more deadly than Crowsmirth in a few hours. We'll wear our face wrappings. We park away from the main street, so they can't see what we're driving. They might not be able to tell we're the same people."

"You don't give them enough credit," Andrei sighed. "We're still wearing the same clothes. They'll know exactly who we are."

"No, they won't. All of Thomas's people dress like this, remember? This is the uniform he chose for us so we can be anonymous. They won't suspect a thing."

He rubbed his hands together as they stepped over the broken fence. "I hope you're right."

"Me too," she said.

Kit took one last look at her broken home before turning her back on it for good. "I'm glad we didn't stay," she admitted. "I'm glad to leave it behind." All the same, tears welled in her eyes.

Andrei put an arm around her shoulders. "Remember, you're not alone anymore, okay? You have us. We'll get through it together."

She sniffed and nodded, wiping at her eyes. "I'm glad you all found me."

"Me too," Mercy admitted. She allowed herself a small smile. They had a long road ahead of them, and a long night to follow. Hundreds of werewolves. The thought send a shiver down her spine and she walked a little faster.

———

THEY KEPT a quick pace heading back to the Tortoise hidden in the small clearing. The shadows were already getting long and Mercy was grateful they were heading into Crowsmirth instead of Kanta. She honestly didn't think they would make it back to Kanta before nightfall, and she would feel better being in civilization when the hundreds of werewolves descended. Even if that town was a wreck, it was better than being caught in the woods.

The three of them piled into the Tortoise, moving quickly since the forest had gotten dark during their walk back. Mercy hopped in to sit shotgun while Andrei got into the driver's seat. Kit settled in the back, marveling at the vehicle.

"I thought you were joking when you called it a Tortoise, but it really does have that armored feel." She smiled while buckling in. Mercy passed her water and one of the granola bars before helping Andrei eat some. He had to be careful while he drove through the underbrush. She nibbled on some too, though she felt too nervous to eat much. She knew she needed the calories for energy.

Despite the bumpy terrain, Andrei got them turned around and back on the road. Thank goodness the Tortoise was bottom heavy so it wouldn't tip over. In the distance the sun sank toward the horizon far faster than Mercy liked. Why hadn't they gone on this mission in the summer when the days felt endless?

It had taken them longer than the estimated half an hour to get back to the Tortoise, mostly because she and Andrei had wandered in circles before stumbling upon Kit's home. Yes, they found their way back, but Mercy kicked herself for not marking trees as they went. It would have made returning faster. Now they suffered because of it. She could practically feel time slipping away from them as the large wheels kicked up dirt and Andrei gunned it for Crowsmirth.

To keep from badgering Andrei and making him nervous as he drove, Mercy focused on Kit. She needed a better disguise. Yes, she was in the tunic, but it was still clear she was a girl. Mercy directed her how to wrap down her chest to give her a boyish look. Kit had to lean forward so Mercy could help her with the face wrappings. They had a pile of them in case theirs came to pieces, and she was glad they had prepared at least that much. Mercy took careful attention with the wrappings around Kit's head, hiding her short black hair as much as possible. Kit had been to Crowsmirth before which meant she could be recognized if they weren't careful.

"It's best not to talk while we're out. You could give yourself away," Mercy said as the seats bounced beneath them. Andrei maneuvered the Tortoise carefully over the bridge before hitting the road again. "Pretend you're mute if you have to, and let Andrei and I do the talking. These people know you exist, or at least know of you. So even talking could give you away."

"Okay," Kit whispered. Her awe at riding in the Tortoise was gone, replaced with a nervousness Mercy knew well. She sat as still as she could despite her quick breaths. She had been chased out of Crowsmirth the last time she tried to enter the city, nearly captured by traffickers. That had to be terrifying, but it didn't come close to the werewolves that could soon descend on the city.

Out of all of them, Kit was the only one who knew what was coming for them come nightfall. She knew the numbers they would face if they didn't make it in time. Hundreds of werewolves. Mercy's hands shook as she worked, but she tried not to focus on that. She tried instead to pay attention to the task at hand: making sure Kit was properly disguised, making sure Kit was safe.

Without warning, Andrei gasped. Mercy had just enough time to turn toward him to see what was going on when the Tortoise slung to the side and slipped into the woods, flinging Kit and Mercy from their seats. Mercy hit the door, her head nearly going out the open window. Kit was still buckled in, but since she was in the middle, she just got flung to the side. Mercy pulled herself out of the door.

She cried, "What the hell?"

The vehicle went down into a ditch before nosing up a hill again and stopping just in front of a clump of bushes. Mercy took a moment to catch her breath and Kit let out a weak sigh from the back seat. Mercy was shaking. She turned to Andrei.

"What was that all about?" she snapped at him.

"Sorry, I panicked," he said, his voice shaky and breathless. His hands were still on the steering wheel and shaking. Slowly, he leaned his head back and she could see terror in his eyes. "You okay back there, Kit?"

"Yeah," Kit said softly. "I'm fine."

Andrei swallowed hard. "There were hunters. Lots of them. They were right at the bend. I saw them and… I freaked out and panicked. I'm sorry. Without really thinking, I spotted this place and darted for it. Damn it, I hope you both aren't hurt."

"Not hurt, just rattled," Mercy admitted.

"Good." Andrei swallowed and finally sat up straighter in his seat. "I think I lost a couple years off my life with that one." He gave a nervous chuckle.

Hunters.

Mercy clenched her jaw. That was the last thing they needed right now. Andrei was still in danger if they found out what he was, and Kit could be captured if they knew she was a girl. She had no training and possibly very little experience around people. It was risky enough going to Crowsmirth when it was practically deserted with fresh corpses about, but it would be even worse if a bunch of nosy hunters got involved.

Kit was probably the most vulnerable of them all. She would have a hard time passing if they questioned her. She had no trial runs in this disguise and didn't even fully understand the work at the mill to parrot it back if asked. In so many ways, she was like Mercy growing up, isolated and alone save for an abusive family. Working at a home base, with a slew of chores to keep her too busy to question, too busy to escape. And of course, always restricted from leaving even to go into town. Mercy's naivety had almost gotten her killed. She couldn't let the same thing happen to Kit.

No, this wasn't the time to go down that path and reopen those memories. That would have to wait for another time. She needed to focus on the present, keep herself grounded on what they needed now. Her friends needed her. She looked out the windows. The woods were even darker than before. That meant the hundreds of werewolves wouldn't be far behind. Mercy knew what she needed to do. Both Andrei and Kit relied on her. They needed her to take charge, even though she was terrified.

"What are hunters doing out here?" Kit asked, undoing her seatbelt and sitting forward. "Did they come to kill the werewolves?" Kit didn't sound excited, but suspicious. Mercy couldn't give her a clear answer, not yet. Not until she saw what they were up to.

"I guess we'll figure that out together. Come on."

She grabbed the door handle and shoved it open. "Let's get moving. We don't have much time. Grab the essentials." She used the deeper voice that had once fooled Jacob Pillsby, the sheriff of Kanta. Kit blinked in confusion for a moment, but she followed Mercy's request and hopped out of the backseat. Andrei was still reeling. He gave her a confused expression, at first, before understanding dawned on him and he crawled out too. His legs were shaking.

They were going to need a miracle to pull this off.

Mercy and Andrei left behind their Wolves of Kanta helmets and instead made sure their own disguises were secured. They wrapped up their faces quickly with practiced speed, much to Kit's surprise. Then Mercy grabbed their trail mix and their flasks of water. She checked on the leather pouch on her thigh to make sure the needles were still there. At least those were still in place.

"Are those to help the werewolves?" Kit asked, watching her closely.

Mercy nodded. "If we have no way out, this is an option. It's a dangerous option," she admitted, "but it's better than nothing."

Kit gave a slow nod and let out a shaky breath.

Mercy gave Andrei his water flask and shut the door to the vehicle. She looked each of them over. Kit looked to the world like an amateur hunter from Farrell Mill, maybe somebody's son learning the path of their father. What Mercy could have been to her father. That would be a good angle.

"How far are the hunters?" she asked Andrei.

Andrei shifted uncomfortably. "Oh, uh, just around the bend… sir."

Mercy stood straighter, taking on the posture of her father by looping her left thumb into the belt of her pants and hovered her right hand over her gun. "Good. Kipper," she said to Kit. "Keep close. You have a lot of training to do still."

Kit snickered before quickly falling back into composure again under Mercy's glare. She cleared her throat before giving a stern nod. Good, this was not the time for games.

"Remember," Mercy looked to each of them. "Let me do the talking."

They both nodded. Mercy got the impression neither of them wanted to do any talking with hunters. That was good because Mercy was still figuring out a story for them.

PART 3

THE LONG NIGHT

8

CHOKE POINT

TOGETHER THE THREE made their way through the broken underbrush left in the wake of the Tortoise slamming through the forest and returned to the road on foot. Mercy could only imagine what they looked like to onlookers, a trio of hunters from Farrell Mill emerging from the woods so close to nightfall. It would be hard to explain, especially since one of them was clearly still learning the ropes. She swallowed down her nerves, determined again to take on her father's composure.

They stepped out onto the dirt road, avoiding the weeds on either side of the wheel tracks, and made their way toward Crowsmirth. The sun was a sliver over the horizon and a cold breeze gave her goosebumps.

Sure enough, the hunters had made a traffic stop just as the street turned toward Crowsmirth. Multiple vehicles blockaded the road and around the street they had traps and barricades up. Mercy had never seen such a high level of organization before.

Rope traps linked from the trees to the ground. Vehicles were sideways along the road with giant, metal spikes protruding out of their sides. At least twenty hunters, all fully armed with likely silver ammunition, milled about behind them, rifles at their sides. She didn't blame Andrei for being terrified. This was a show of force. She glanced over to him, amazed to see he didn't show any hesitation. He walked with the same authoritative stance as Mercy. Her heart swelled for him. He was being so brave, and she loved him for it.

Looking back at the setup the hunters had made, Mercy understood what this strange formation was: a choke point.

Her father had mentioned them to her before, but he'd been dismissive of their effectiveness. He had been ripped off by a few groups he had tried to work with in the past, but in her father's true fashion, he had decided that they were all full of lying, cheating hunters looking for suckers to convince to be bait. The irony of him using that as an insult, while simultaneously training Mercy to serve as bait, wasn't lost on her, even as a child. His hypocrisy had nagged at her even then in her formative years. Sure, they bagged a lot of werewolves, but the danger of working all night for a meager cut had made him sour. The chance of survival, he had admitted once after too many drinks, made it the most dangerous way of life for a hunter. Leaders never were transparent about the numbers until the end of a hunt and come morning, there were always a few dead hunters. That was the unspoken goal, he told her. The fewer hunters alive come morning, the fewer ways they had to split the proceeds. Drunken brawls were common. Supposed accidental deaths were also common. Bad leadership usually meant a high turnover. The dead hunters would often be used as bait if they were doing a sting operation for multiple days.

Anything Mercy had imagined from her father's late night drunken stories was so much smaller than the reality before her. She hadn't imagined they would barricade the road. That didn't make any sense to her, considering the werewolves wouldn't be driving. Or was everyone a suspicious person? Was it just an excuse to harass and question any stranger on the road during the day? Considering some of them were likely traffickers, that quite logical thought made her shiver.

On the opposite side of the street, the side that headed toward Kanta, stood another blockade. They had cut off any traffic that planned to pass through Crowsmirth. Everyone had to stop at the city before moving forward. She, Andrei, and Kit, couldn't have gotten through if they had tried to drive back to Kanta —and it would have not only blown their cover, but Thomas's cover too. Mercy took a deep breath to calm her nerves. She only hoped they had made the right decision to stay.

As they approached the blockade, Mercy held up a hand to one man seated in a vehicle. He was drinking from a clay bowl of something hot.

He took one long slurp, spilling some on his black beard, before he looked at her with drunken eyes.

"What's going on here?" she asked in her attempt at a deep voice.

He shrugged. "Men died last night. Bunch of werewolves came through. They say over a hundred, but you know how people talk sometimes. I'll believe it when I see it, you know?" He grunted a laugh before returning to his bowl. Kit squirmed beside her, but she didn't say a word. Mercy was proud of her.

Clearly this man didn't care what they did, which was a relief. She turned to Kit, but glanced to Andrei to let them know she was addressing both of them.

"Now this is what they call a blockade. You'll see the various traps here…" She described a few of the traps, mostly to keep them from accidentally getting snagged in one.

Kit nodded attentively, but Mercy saw she was trembling from head to toe. She didn't blame her, going from near isolation to this. Mercy was having to put on a show, but inside she felt the same as Kit: terrified.

Andrei was clearly sweating and although he sounded chill with his words, his eyes were wide and his hands were shoved into his pockets. She doubted he had ever known about any of these things when he was living in his pack, but now he understood what he and his friends had been up against. It was horrific. Mercy knew the ins and outs of everything. She just hoped this didn't change his perspective of her.

"Alright, I think that's good enough for now," Mercy said with the best impression of her father she could muster, even hiking up her belt buckle afterwards. "Let's see if we can find a bed for the night so we can watch the parade."

She turned to lead them through the barricade and saw the man in the vehicle smiling at them. He tipped his hat to Mercy. "I remember those good old days, taking my first steps as a werewolf hunter. I couldn't wait to watch those heads roll!"

Andrei crossed his arms and Mercy hoped he wasn't going to say anything, but the man was too drunk to notice.

He held out a hand. "The name is Davidson. Yours?"

"Mark." Mercy shook his hand, squeezing tight and hoping with all her being he wasn't suspicious of anything.

"Make sure they have good seats for tonight," he said with absolute glee. Mercy felt her stomach drop at his words. "It's going to be a bloodbath!"

Even knowing what was at stake and the danger she was putting them all in, Mercy couldn't bring herself to respond. She couldn't find the words. Her mind went blank every time she tried to think of something to say. Instead, seeing the brief confusion on his face, she turned away from Davidson and led Andrei and Kit through the blockade.

She wanted to scream so badly she could feel the sound in the back of her throat demanding to be released. If they had been faster, if they had left the mill earlier, if they had explained things to Kit more quickly, maybe lives would be saved tonight. It would be a bloodbath of innocent lives. How many of them were her age? How many of them would be young children?

Her thighs hurt from pressing her fingertips into them at her sides. She hummed to herself to keep the scream from being released, to keep herself and her friends safe.

"Excuse me, mister?" Someone called from the barricade. It wasn't Davidson, and Mercy had a sinking feeling.

"What is it?" she asked, allowing the scream to turn into her father's annoyed growl instead. "Can't you see I'm training over here?"

It was someone she didn't recognize. The man was tall, muscular, and had white hair. He also had a black eye patch over his left eye. She looked over his expensive but hardy clothes and the well-kept weapons. He was a seasoned werewolf hunter, likely someone who went on many of these outings. He had her father's calm menacing presence that told her he was likely good at his job and could kill a man without a single care. Mercy's stomach twisted in knots. "Sorry to interrupt," he said in a terse voice. "But all entries into Crowsmirth have to be tested."

Mercy snorted. "Tested? What the hell."

The man pulled out what at first looked like a fireplace poker. But when the light hit it, it shone white. Andrei hissed in a breath. If she hadn't been standing beside him, she wouldn't have heard it. That's when she knew exactly what it was. Silver.

"I'm sorry, sir, but we have to test all travelers." He gave an annoyed smile. "That's what the barricade is for, after all."

Mercy clammed up. She shouldn't have, she should have kept talking, kept it moving, danced her way out of the conversation completely, but her mind started whirling. Silver. Would that hurt Andrei? Would it kill him? She thought back to the blood experiments. To the iterations she had done again and again, before falling onto the batch she ultimately gave to him. That had made him resistant to silver, didn't it? She hadn't tested it outside of a Petri dish. She hadn't had the chance. No, she hadn't had the nerve. She hadn't wanted to try it for fear of losing him. Now here she was, surrounded by hunters, being forced into testing it here, on the spot.

"Sure," Andrei said in an incredibly calm voice.

Mercy's stared daggers into his back as he stepped toward the man. What was he doing?

"What's your name again?" Andrei asked. "I'm still learning and I'm trying to get a feel for who everybody is around here." He was fiddling with something, maybe his sleeve as he pulled off a glove.

"Malik," the older man stated, clearly impatient. "I manage the perimeter. It extends all around this city, and all wanderers or hunters who come in here have a simple silver test. That includes you three."

"Sure, sure. Sorry," Andrei bit the tip of his glove and pulled it off. Then reached forward and grabbed the silver rod.

Mercy's heart skipped a beat. She couldn't breathe. She half expected him to fall to the ground.

His hand couldn't have been on it a second before he pulled his hand back with a cry. Mercy jumped, holding back the urge to rush toward him. Malik took a step back in surprise.

Andrei held up his hand, showing blood dripping

down his palm. "That thing's sharp! Dang, you could have warned me!"

"I'm… sorry." Malik's words were stilted. "I didn't mean to harm you. We just needed to make sure."

Andrei gripped his hand to his chest, wincing. "Yeah well, as you can see it isn't burned. Just bleeding is all! Just great, right when a bunch of werewolves enter the city."

Malik grumbled in annoyance. "Look, I'm sorry about that, but this is protocol!"

"Can your protocol hurry it up so we can get a room then, Malik?" Mercy snapped.

Clearly rattled, Malik went to test Mercy next. She hiked up her glove an inch and pressed the back of her arm against the bar. It was cold to the touch and was indeed sharp. Had it really cut Andrei that easily though?

Kit watched Mercy's motions and did the same, touching the blade with her pinkie finger before putting it back in her pocket.

"Good. You're all fine to proceed. Again… sorry for the inconvenience." He turned back to the barricade. Mercy and Kit huddled over Andrei.

"What the hell were you thinking?" Mercy hissed at him. "You could have been killed!"

"I didn't touch it, okay? I had to do something. They wouldn't have let us come in otherwise."

Mercy took his hand and pulled it close. He was cut pretty deep, to where he was bleeding. She sighed and pulled out cloth wrappings to bind it. They weren't clean like they should be, but they couldn't be picky.

"That was brilliant," Kit whispered. "Did you cut yourself beforehand? I thought you really got cut by it."

"Good, that was the goal," Andrei said. "If I touched it, I didn't know what would happen. Even if all I did was faint or something, that would have made them kick us out. Or worse. I couldn't let that happen, not this close to nightfall. Besides, it'll heal quick."

Mercy finished wrapping it and met his gaze. She wanted to pull down those bandages and kiss him. Maybe slap him, but definitely kiss him too. "Never frighten me like that again."

His eyes glinted with a smile. "Hey, we got through it, okay? We passed the test. I'm fine."

She resisted the urge to put a hand to his cheek, to wrap an arm around his waist, to do anything to assuage the desire within to let him know that she cared. She wanted to touch him to remind herself that he really was fine, but she couldn't. They couldn't do anything to draw more attention than they already had.

She hated these damn disguises, and she hated these hunters.

MERCY LOOKED AROUND THEM, focusing on Crowsmirth instead of her own emotions. It was difficult forcing herself to stay in the moment instead of getting stuck in her head again. The barricade wasn't just on the road in and out of Crowsmirth, it made a complete perimeter around the town, like Malik had said. There would be no escape until morning. If one section of the barricade went down, there were backup vehicles to take its place. To be honest, this was probably the safest place to be outside of the mill.

As much as she hated to admit it, Andrei was right. His impromptu acting had been incredibly dangerous, but they had nowhere else to go until morning. If he hadn't done that, they now could be imprisoned or dead.

The general store was dark and the doorway and windows had been boarded up. She wondered if they had buried the grocer's body or if they were using it to lure the hundreds of werewolves into their trap. As much as she wanted the man's body to be shown some kind of respect, she also knew the old adage: other than women, the best bait for a werewolf was a dead human.

Across the street, the building that had the mad shooter that morning was now also dark and boarded up. Good. She hoped that man had been removed from town and taken far away from here. She could sleep easier knowing no one was in town who might recognize them. They could not afford unwanted attention right now, especially in a place that felt ready to explode.

"Hey, uh, Mark?"

She blinked and turned to Andrei, putting her hands behind her back like Thomas sometimes did. "Yes, Andy?"

A smile came to his eyes again, but he cleared his throat. He pointed to the inn, the only building along the entire road that looked even a little occupied. One oil lantern flickered, hanging by the door. "Um, how much do you think it'll be to stay there?"

Cursing under her breath, her chest suddenly felt tight. Money. The one thing she could never look at let alone touch when she lived with her father. Something she never needed at the mill. She had forgotten all about money.

"I have no clue," she whispered, pleading with her eyes. "I have nothing on me. Um, Kipper?"

Kit gave a nervous yelp and shook her head. She was breathing hard, probably panicking. Mercy wasn't sure if she was going to cry or wanted to hide somewhere.

Andrei held up his hands. "Okay, don't worry, I'll take care of it."

"What?" Mercy asked, trying to figure out his plan from studying his eyes. He held her gaze, mischief in his eyes. What was he on about? Since when did he have money?

"Trust me?"

Mercy felt her own hands shaking. It was different when she was the leader and knew the plan. She could trust herself to bluff her way through things, but she reminded herself, she had just seen Andrei was more than capable of it too. He was so good even she had been fooled. But she was still anxious.

He glided past her and Mercy had to resist the urge to reach a hand out to take his hand, to find reassurance in his closeness, in his grip. But doing that was far too dangerous. She needed to stop those urges. It could get them killed here.

Following Andrei's lead, Mercy and Kit stayed close

behind him as he opened the inn door and stepped inside.

The place was dark compared to the dwindling light outside along with all the lit torches. It took a moment for her eyes to adjust. It smelled musty, as if in desperate need of a good deep cleaning and a few open windows. She caught the scent of a cigar and spotted a room off to the side where several hunters were in deep discussion. She only heard snippets of their words, all about tactics and locations. These men had to be the leaders of this hunting party. They had been the ones to implement the choke point. While their men stayed on the ground outside, they sat in the inn's comfort, drinking, and smoking and postulating in the dark.

Old fools, her father used to call them. For once she had to agree with him.

Andrei spoke to an old man behind the counter, who pulled out a ledger book. Abruptly, words from the leaders made her blood run cold.

"Three girls may not be enough, what if we need more bait?"

For a moment, the world tilted and Mercy feared she would collapse to the floor. They were using girls as bait. The memory came back to her in a sudden rush.

Golden eyes in the darkness. The she-wolf leaping in the air toward her. Her father's gun cocking in the still night air as he screamed at her to run.

If her father was still alive, would that have been her fate as well? Would she have been turned into bait for hundreds of werewolves while these men sat safely in their den? Her father might not have taken part in the enormous werewolf hunts again, but he certainly wasn't against using his daughter for profit. In fact, he talked about it so much that she had been eager to put herself in danger. She had been eager to be used as bait, much like those girls outside probably were.

Mercy shuddered. Her breathing came in short, rapid bursts. The candlelight swirled in her vision. She had always known that was the purpose, right? Why was it so much more upsetting hearing that it was happening to a group of girls? Why did it make her entire body quake to realize she could have been used as bait for *hundreds* of werewolves?

She closed her eyes, focused on her breathing, and willed her hands to stop shaking. She had been so naïve then. No, she argued with herself, she had been a child who trusted her father. Too many questions at home had gotten her a beating. She grew up knowing she would be used as bait to bring more werewolves in, but she never questioned where he got the idea from. She never questioned who else he might have seen be used as bait. Mercy had been eager to help, anything to get his approval. Even if it meant baiting a werewolf. Had he hoped for that? He had mentioned multiple times how his job would be easier once she was old enough to be bait. He talked about bringing in more money, bagging more werewolves, upgrading their home. It would never have worked, Mercy knew the truth now. But that didn't take away the horror of it.

Those girls out there in the woods would face down the hundreds of werewolves on their way. None of them would likely survive the night, but they believed they were helping. They thought they were being useful to the hunters in bringing down the monsters, but they were really throwing away their lives. If things had been different, Mercy would have done the same.

Slowly the dread that had almost toppled her to the ground transformed into something different. Her shaky hands turned to fists. Her breathing calmed and her jaw clenched. Anger filled her heart fueled by her childhood naivety, her father's cruelty, and the dangerous lies that led to women dying simply to draw in werewolves. It was such a waste of life.

Mercy had no outlet for her rage. Not here, not yet. Once again she had to push down her anger and turn her back on the faceless leaders in the room, the ones choosing to sacrifice so many others to make themselves wealthier. Instead, she opened her eyes and focused on the man behind the counter.

He hunched over his desk. With thinning black hair a little overgrown around his pale face, he frowned as Andrei pulled coins from his pocket. The man's gaze moved over the three of them, fixing on Mercy for a moment longer than the rest.

"There you go, hopefully that's all you need," Andrei said, clasping his hands.

The man pinched his lips together, counted the coins, and clicked his tongue in thought. Yes, keeping her mind on their mission helped Mercy remain calm. It kept her from wanting to scream at the top of her lungs and rush into that back room to shake those supposed leaders. Slowly she unclenched her jaw and relaxed her fists, feeling her palms throb after relaxing her fingers.

The man glanced to a list on a wall and dragged a finger down the yellowed paper. "Yes, it looks like we do have some rooms available. I assume you three gentlemen want separate quarters?"

Mercy blinked. Was that her imagination or did he emphasize the word *gentlemen*? Mercy glanced to Kit and Andrei, but they hadn't seemed to notice. Nothing was off or out of place. She shook herself, wondering if her anger was making her overly suspicious.

"One room is fine," Andrei said.

Andrei leaned against the counter, his hip jutted out to the side and made his pants look slightly tighter. That was an excellent distraction, Mercy decided with a smirk.

"We'll manage," Andrei added.

The man furrowed his brows but didn't give a retort. Good, because with the mood Mercy was in, it wouldn't last long. He gave several coins back to Andrei then pulled out a quill to mark on the paper on the wall.

"Name?" The old man asked without looking at them.

"Farrell," Andrei said. "My friend and I are in training to work there soon. This seems like the best place to learn about being a werewolf hunter considering how many we're expected to have, am I right?"

He gave Andrei a long look before frowning and marking on the page. "I wouldn't know much about werewolves," he drawled.

Andrei was good at lying on the spot when the pressure came on. Where the heck had he learned that? Was it from working as an apprentice at the apothecary, or when he was a guard for his pack? Either way, Mercy was grateful. She would have to pick his brain for details later.

It was interesting how much disdain people felt for Thomas and his mill. Mercy wasn't sure if it was because of envy, or distaste about how he conducted his work. Her father hadn't ever spoken about the gossip of the town or where it came from. He hadn't put much faith in that, but then again, he hadn't told her much about things outside of being a werewolf hunter.

Following another piercing look at each of them, the man finally slid a large brass key across the table. Andrei took it and read the number scrawled on the paper tag.

"That's… the top floor?"

"Yes. I'm sure it will give you an excellent view of the spectacle tonight." He managed a small smile, but it looked forced. Mercy couldn't decide if he disliked them or if it was something else, but it nagged at her.

Andrei nodded and thanked the man before heading toward the stairs. Kit followed close behind him, but Mercy lingered behind. Once Andrei and Kit were out of earshot, she approached the table.

"You don't approve of all this, do you?" She spoke in a conspiratorial voice, keeping her gaze steady.

He glanced to her with a bloodshot gaze of contempt she hadn't expected. Then just as quickly his expression shifted into something closer to apathy. Mercy's heart pounded harder in her chest, but she kept her expression relaxed and conspiratorial. She couldn't give away what she felt inside. It took him a moment to respond, as though he was too stunned to talk.

"Whatever it takes to rid this land of these animals."

It was recited, a phrase he clearly had spoken so many times that the meaning of it was now lost, along with any conviction he might have once felt.

Mercy thought back to the body of the grocer she had found across the street that morning, covered in crows. The man didn't look like the one who had shot at her that morning—that man had been younger, more animated. However, he seemed far too calm to have lived through the bloodbath that must have rocked Crowsmirth the night before. He clearly had come in from elsewhere, perhaps taking advantage of the influx of visitors and the lack of an innkeeper to make some additional money. He held disdain, but she wasn't sure if it was for the slaughter that would come this night, or if it was aimed at the three of them. Regardless, it was the opposite of the exuberant energy that came from the hunters. For them, this was a celebration.

She opened her mouth, intending to delve further, but heavy footfalls behind her made her turn.

The men in the meeting room had started filing out through the front door. Whatever battle plans or bait they had put together was about to put into action. That meant they had little time before the werewolves descended.

"You had best get upstairs," the man said. She turned back to see he held a few wooden boards in one hand and a hammer in the other. He went around the counter and Mercy noticed the heavy limp he had. "It's almost dark. I have to board up the front door. Hopefully, it will keep them out tonight."

Mercy doubted it, but she couldn't tell him that. "Do you need any help?"

He propped the boards against the wall. He was stronger than he looked. "At my age, I never say no to help."

She nodded and shut the front door then held the boards as he nailed each of them into place. They worked in silence for a long time, getting three boards up before he said, "You can call me Oscar." He hammered in the last nail. "Thank you for your help."

"No problem," she said. "You had better find some cover, Oscar. It's going to be bad tonight." She turned for the stairs when he called over to her.

"And your name?"

Mercy paused, glancing back to him. "Mer—Mark." Her cheeks flushed, hoping he hadn't noticed her slip-up.

"Of course it is." He grinned. His smile gave Mercy pause. "Take care of your trainees. It's going to be a bloody night." He picked up his tools and headed back to the counter.

Mercy nodded and pushed aside her embarrassment. She didn't have time to say more. She hurried up the four floors to reach the top. Andrei and Kit had left the door cracked. Quickly she stepped inside and closed and latched the door behind her.

"WE WERE worried you wouldn't make it," Kit said. She was perched by the window on an old, wooden chair still wearing her complete disguise.

Andrei had been pacing, but pulled Mercy into a wordless hug as soon as she closed the door behind her. He squeezed her so tight she couldn't breathe for a bit, but she didn't mind. She pulled away and his gorgeous caramel eyes searched hers.

"We have the biggest pack of werewolves we've ever encountered about to bear down on this town and you thought it was a good time to chit chat with the innkeeper?" His eyes crinkled with a smile, but he still gripped her elbows with desperate worry.

She reached up and placed a hand to his cheek. "I wasn't chatting. I was helping him board up the front door."

He shook his head and released his grip. "That's about what I expected. Next time, don't help people, okay?" He paused and swallowed before continuing, "I don't want to lose you."

"After tonight, I don't know if that man will even be alive. You saw what this place looked like this morning. I have a feeling Oscar knows something. He's suspicious but I don't know why. I don't think he likes all these hunters here, and I'm curious about it."

He laughed and shook his head. "You're in a town surrounded by hunters. Everybody is suspicious here."

"Fair." Mercy grinned as she peeled off her head bandages, grateful to let her skin breathe.

"Are you sure that's a good idea?" Kit asked. "I mean, what if someone sees us?"

"They would have to climb up four stories to see anything. I think we deserve a breather for a moment." At her prompting, Kit and Andrei removed their wrappings as well. Kit took longer to remove hers, but she relaxed into her chair after.

As helpful as the face wrappings were, Mercy was afraid they would get in the way during a fight. Werewolves were their biggest threat now.

"I don't know how you all deal with those all the time," Kit admitted, pocketing her wrappings after seeing Mercy and Andrei do the same.

"Practice." Mercy smirked. "Andrei, how is your hand. Can I see?"

He pulled off his glove and held out his hand. Mercy angled his palm so she could see it from the light coming in from the window. The cut he had made earlier was completely gone from what she could see. Only the bloodstains on the wrappings showed there had ever been a wound.

"Did the silver touch you at all?"

"No," he said. "I didn't actually touch it. Not with all those hunters around." He gave a nervous laugh. "I told you this before. Don't you believe me?"

"I know, I just… I worry about you. A lot."

"I know." He picked up her hand and kissed it. "I think it's cute."

She shook her head. "I'm glad somebody appreciates it."

They were distracted by the loud sound of Kit dragging two chairs over to the window. "Can you two cut it out and help me watch for them? We didn't get this room for you two to have mushy time together."

Mercy caught Andrei's gaze, they both smiled. Andrei chuckled and Mercy shook her head. Then they both made their way to their chairs near the window.

"It's weird to see so many of those hunters congregated in one place like this. Is it normal?" Kit asked.

Mercy plopped down onto her seat beside her. "If there's enough money to go around, they'll go wherever they can. I bet a bunch of them are novices though. I doubt many of them have much experience around werewolves, but the potential money makes people do ridiculous things."

As Mercy's eyes adjusted to the darkness of the room and the pitch black, cloudy sky outside, she could see the hunters outside. They congregated around the oil lanterns and the vehicles. They would be easily spotted by werewolves too. A few of the leaders from the meeting downstairs were still wandering off to their posts.

Mercy thought back to when she wandered into Kanta later than she should have and ran into Henry transformed as a werewolf. These leaders should have been in their places hours ago. Of course, they might not fully grasp the sheer numbers they were up against. They probably thought it was all talk. Davidson had said they were supposed to get over a hundred werewolves, but Mercy trusted Kit's estimation of hundreds instead. She was the one who had been on the ground, seeing them night after night. These people were grossly outnumbered and they no idea. Not yet.

Looking at all the hunters from a werewolf's perspective, it wasn't a blockade, but a feast. Just glancing through she saw dozens of weak spots, and if she could see them, then the werewolves would find them. If they could clamor over an electrified fence to get into Kit's house, they could easily get over these vehicles, traps, and blockades. A few would be killed or trapped, sure, but it wouldn't stem the tide. This was going to backfire horribly.

"How many do you think there are?" Kit asked, her voice wavering. Mercy glanced to her, noticing how she sat straight-backed in her chair, almost leaning out the window. She was terrified. Mercy swallowed down the dry patch in her throat, realizing Kit was right to call her and Andrei out for being distracted earlier. This was hardly the best time.

"Maybe a hundred hunters… if I'm being generous. I heard more behind the inn as we came inside." Andrei thumbed over his shoulder. "It's a lot of hunters, sure, but…" He shook his head.

They were all thinking the same thing.

Kit turned to look at him, her eyes wide and her voice trembling. "It isn't going to be enough, is it? We'll either watch the hunters be slaughtered or the werewolves get butchered." She hung her head. "This is so pointless! If you all could have gotten to the pack today instead of wasting your time on me, then maybe all these people wouldn't die tonight!"

Mercy reached out to her, but she turned back to the window, her fingers curling as she gripped the wooden armrests of her chair.

"Please, don't talk like that," she urged. "If it weren't for you, we might have tried staying in the Tortoise overnight. We wouldn't have survived the night, Kit."

Kit shook her head. "I know, you're right. Sorry, I guess I'm just nervous. I've never seen a werewolf attack from outside of my cage." She wiped tears away from her cheeks. "I kind of miss that cage right now."

Mercy gave a sad smile. "I kind of want a cage to curl up in tonight too. Don't feel bad."

Andrei scooted his chair over and wrapped an arm around Mercy's shoulders. She couldn't resist leaning her head against him, grateful for his presence.

"If the werewolves get through—" his breath was warm against her ear "—do you think we'll be safe up here?"

"Honestly? I don't know. I think Crowsmirth is the safest place outside of the mill, and this inn is probably one of the safest places here. It's boarded up downstairs, so that will help if they get past the barricade."

"They will get past," Kit said ominously. "There are too many weak spots, and these werewolves are smart." She got to her feet and started pointing them out. Mercy had already seen them, but Andrei clearly got more nervous as Kit spoke. "They're going to swarm this place."

Mercy's eyes went wide. One of the hunters in the distance ran toward the trees, his rifle only partially raised at his side. She pushed away from Andrei.

"Kit, sit down," she muttered.

Kit paused and glanced to her with wide eyes. "What?"

"Sit down and don't move, either of you."

Kit did as she was told.

The hunter disappeared into the woods. His rifle flared. In the distance, a scream rang out before being cut short.

"They're here," Mercy whispered.

9

———

THE INN

SCREAMS ECHOED THROUGHOUT CROWSMIRTH. Up and down the barricade, rifle shots blasted through the chill night air. The weak points Kit had pointed out lit up like fireworks with the crack of gunfire. Already the defensive setup was no match for the assault. The hunters weren't nearly as prepared as they should have been.

Most of the assault from their vantage point was hitting the blockade where they had briefly spoken with Davidson. The drunken hunter had scoffed at the idea of a hundred werewolves but if what they saw from this small section of the assault was any sign of the numbers they were facing, Kit hadn't been exaggerating. Mercy put a hand to the pouch filled with dipped needles still slung against her hip. Even if they had found one campsite, she hadn't brought nearly enough of her cure. There really had been no way to prevent this.

One of the massive trucks was shoved back and spun to the side like a toy.

Andrei kept his voice low. "Did werewolves do that, or was that from an explosion? How are they so strong?"

Mercy reached over and took his hand. He was shaking. "They must be working together somehow."

She thought back to the electric fence at Kit's old home. The way the werewolves had disabled the barricade, not seeming to care if they sacrificed some of their own. It had worked and they took on very few losses because of it. She wasn't sure if it was calculated or just a fluke, but now this was different. One werewolf couldn't have flipped that truck. Yes, a single werewolf was strong, but they couldn't shove a vehicle like that. They had to be teaming up.

Large sections of the forest around Crowsmirth had become eerily silent. No more gunshots lit up the trees in those gaps, and that made Mercy nervous. Those forces were probably dead, and the werewolves were moving into the city. That concerned her. Likely the werewolves surrounded the city too. They weren't all coming from the road, but from all parts. Were there several camps spread around the woods, or had the transformed werewolves thought that far ahead?

People ran from the barricades on the street. They didn't make it far before werewolves leaped out of the trees and landed on top of them. None of them could escape. The barricade even made it easier for the werewolves to catch up to the humans, almost corralling them together like sheep to the slaughter.

Kit curled up in her chair, covering her mouth with her hands as she whimpered. Andrei stared in open horror at the sight, shaking from head to toe. Mercy looked to her friends, looked to the open window, and realized the danger. They were caught up in the carnage just like she had been, but they needed to move. She needed to lead them. They needed her to step forward and give them a direction to take. All the same, she struggled to pull herself away from the bloodbath and find her voice again.

She finally forced out through a hoarse throat, "We need to move." She swallowed, forcing herself to speak again. "They're looking for prey and we don't want to lure them up here."

Kit glanced at her with wide, tearful eyes, then shot to her feet. Mercy tried to reach out for her, but Kit was too fast.

"Kit—no! Don't move so quickly, they'll be drawn up here!"

But Kit didn't seem to hear her. Clearly in her own world, her actions were governed by the panic induced urgency that had saved her life every night for three months. Scrambling without a word into the back corner of the room, she crouched down to the floor and stared wordlessly at the window with tears streaking her cheeks.

This was too much for her, Mercy realized. Kit had already faced so many horrors, and yet here they were living out probably her worst nightmare.

"Damn, it's too late." Andrei growled. Before Mercy could glance back to the window, Andrei picked her up in his arms and sped across the room. Normally she would be offended being picked up like that, but it meant he didn't have time to explain.

Mercy trusted him to only do it if it was an emergency.

"Did they see us?" Mercy whispered when he sat her down beside Kit who was quaking and whimpering through tears.

"Yeah, at least three did." He picked up the bed with strength and ease that once again surprised her. It wasn't just the mattress, but the entire bed, frame and all. Mercy was speechless as he laid it on its side in front of them, standing it up on its side so that it loomed above their heads. The frame was made of solid hardwood and balanced perfectly as he put it down. The sheets spilled down to their feet, and the pillows fell and landed next to Kit who was near the corner.

Mercy's heart skipped a beat. "Andrei, wait! Don't face them by yourself!"

"I'm not," he whispered, crawling into the gap beside her, taking the side opening and the easy exit.

Mercy put a hand on his shoulder to ease the panic that filled her at the thought he would try to protect them on his own. He wasn't a fool, but the thought of losing him made her chest tight.

"Please don't be a hero, not tonight," she whispered.

He picked up her hand and placed a warm kiss on her knuckles. "It's okay, I don't want to be a hero either." He glanced to the edge of the bed, "Now we have only two access points to protect."

He was right. The bed was on its side and pushed up against the wall, leaving only the top and Andrei's side exposed. Mercy was in the middle and Kit was in the opposite end, curled up in a corner. She had covered herself with the pillows. Her breathing had calmed, so that was good. Mercy didn't want her to go into shock. They needed her alert and ready to move again if the need arose.

Mercy reached over and took her hand. "Kit, are you okay?"

Kit nodded slowly, wiping at her cheeks with her sleeve. "The bed helps. Thanks, Andrei. I'm sorry I messed up." Her voice broke.

Mercy squeezed her hand. "I don't blame you. This is—"

Scraping sounds on the outside of the building took Mercy's thoughts away. All three of them froze with widened eyes. Mercy strained to hear, but at first all she could make out were distant screams. Footsteps padded across the wooden floor, too many of them to merely be one werewolf. The hairs on Mercy's arms stood up. One of the three chairs toppled with a clatter and it sounded like they were snapping at each other. She reached into her holster and pulled out the gun still loaded with silver bullets.

A hand landed on her shoulder and she saw Kit staring at the gun with concern. Kit didn't want her to shoot them. She didn't want her to kill them. To Kit, they couldn't help what they were. Mercy understood that. She also understood blaming yourself for their death if they died. But right now, it was kill them or become their food. There was no other option.

Mercy put a hand on hers and gently pushed it away. She wanted to say it was too late to regret their actions, too late to save the lives of the werewolves who had climbed into their room. At this point, they had to protect themselves. Mercy's hand grazed her satchel full of needles. She glanced down to it, wondering if maybe they could use that. Then she really wouldn't have to kill them.

This time Andrei shook his head at her with fear in his eyes. She blinked at him. He didn't want her to cure them? She searched his gaze for meaning, but he only pleaded with her wordlessly not to do it. If she healed them, could they offer protection from the others? Could they explain to all those hunters out there that these people were not a threat? If they cured one, they could get eaten by the other werewolves in the room. If they chanced changing them all, they might not cooperate. It could blow their cover completely. She doubted the hunters outside would be sympathetic. If the healed werewolves were found out, then Andrei could be found out. She refused to risk him or any of them. The less attention they drew to themselves, the more they could help the rest of the pack.

Mercy turned her attention back to her gun. Kit looked away and curled her arms around herself. Mercy cocked the gun. The silver bullets in the revolving barrel caught the light. She swallowed down the dryness in her throat.

The bed shifted and Mercy heard a werewolf breathing mere feet away from her. They were sniffing around the bed. They could smell them even if they couldn't see them. There was no telling how many of them were in the room. Was it only three like Andrei had seen? It was still possible more had joined. The unknown number made her even more anxious.

Andrei shifted closer to her, his body taut. Even though she carried a gun full of silver, he was still protective of her. It made her heart swell. Despite having incredible strength and so much control over his werewolf transformations, Andrei stood little chance against three fully transformed werewolves. He had to know that.

Mercy looked up, ready to shoot at the first sign of a claw or a muzzle. The mattress shifted as one werewolf placed its forearms on the frame of the bed. Mercy felt her stomach drop as she held the gun up above her head.

More clawed feet clicked on the wooden floor near the window and Mercy winced. There was no telling how many of them were in the room now and she only had five silver bullets. The gun shook in her hands as she tried to keep her focus.

Instead of a muzzle appearing, Mercy heard a snarl beside her. She looked to see Andrei reaching out with a fully formed werewolf arm. His claws ripped across the face of one werewolf, raking across its eye. A bloodied eye darted away from the gap and the unmistakable scent of brimstone struck her nose. Andrei pulled his arm back in quickly as the hulking shadow scrambled backwards with a whimper. She could hear the snorts and huffs of confusion from the others. A crash sounded like one of the wooden chairs had gotten crushed.

That should be a good warning. At least she hoped so. They ought to take the hint and leave. Instead, the others grew more agitated. One of them flung their body at the bed, pushing it closer to the wall, and right up against them. The mattress was thin and did little to keep the springs from poking through. The metal scraped against her arms, but Mercy kept her gun raised and her focus sharp despite the pain.

Straining her ears to hear where they might attack next, Mercy realized Kit was breathing too fast. Mercy glanced to her and saw Kit's face turned to the side. She was in a total panic, but at least she wasn't screaming or whimpering. Mercy wanted to take her hand or pull her into a hug, give her some support, but she couldn't risk it.

Mercy looked up again to see the muzzle of a werewolf come into view. A long gray snout with a black, shiny nose. Its mouth was partially open as if taking in their scent through its mouth. That wasn't a good sign. She tried to aim the gun at its jaws but the mattress was pressing down on her and the springs cut further into her arms, sprouting blood.

The werewolf sniffed the air, then turned its head to the side, pressing its cheek against the wall as it gazed down at her.

Golden eyes met hers. At one point in her life it would have petrified her. Instead, it made her more determined.

The gray werewolf growled, the sound reverberating through the mattress.

"Shoot it," Kit mouthed at her, face pale and waxy.

Beside her, Andrei struck out at another werewolf with his claws, catching it in its cheek. Mercy found her grip, despite the warm blood trickling down her arms, and pulled the trigger.

Kit jumped and Mercy heard Andrei gasp. Holding her breath, Mercy stared at the horrific visage above her.

The werewolf had brought its claws over the edge of the bed, probably intent on pulling the mattress back to reveal its prey. But the bullet struck it just beneath its left eye. The head was flung back and blood splattered against the ceiling. Its paw went limp and slid down on the opposite side of the mattress.

A scurry of clawed feet clambered across the floor of the room before disappearing entirely. Mercy leaned her head back against the wall, covered in sweat and were-wolf blood, gasping for breath as though she had just run a marathon. She looked down at her arms and saw she didn't have many cuts, but they were still bleeding.

"They're gone," Andrei whispered. "The silver gunshot must have scared them off."

"Finally. I thought nothing scared werewolves off," Kit hissed. "Are you sure they're really gone?"

The bed wasn't crushing them against the wall any longer so Mercy shoved it off of them, grateful to no longer have metal digging into her skin.

"If Andrei says they're gone, I believe him," Mercy said. "Come on, we need to get out of here."

"Not like that, you don't." Andrei took some of his wrappings from his pocket. He pulled her close, wrapping the cloth around the wounds on her forearms. The room was dark except for the torches down below throwing shadows up through the window. Andrei's eyes caught the firelight as he bound her arm. She listened to his breathing and appreciated his closeness, wishing she could pull him into an embrace.

"Always taking care of me?" She smiled.

"I try to. You sure do make it difficult."

Kit stepped out from the corner, angling her way around the bed, and hissed in a breath. Mercy glanced in her direction and saw the werewolf's body slumped in the corner. She pulled away from Andrei and brought the gun up, ready to shoot again. But Andrei put a hand on her arm.

"It's okay, it's dead. That's the one you killed."

Mercy's heart thudded in her chest as she stared down at the werewolf that slowly retracted fur and exposed the gleam of skin beneath. Once the fur was gone, she could see that the skull was in pieces and brain matter was splattered up on the walls.

"Damn. So that's what he really looked like," Kit whispered.

Mercy swallowed down the lump in her throat and lowered her gun.

"That's it," Andrei whispered. "Deep breaths." He worked on wrapping her wound again, but she only wanted to pull him to her and never let go. She pushed that impulse away. She didn't have time for that.

"I'm sorry," Mercy whispered to the body at Kit's feet. "I'm sorry you had to die instead of being helped. You deserved better."

Andrei slid his arm around her waist and gave her a hug. "Are you okay?"

She pushed him gently back, nodding. "No, but I

will be." She glanced over to Kit who was crouched down over the body, one hand over her mouth as she stared at the corpse. It was unsettling to see her like that.

Andrei must have seen the state Kit was in because he went over to put an arm under her elbow and pulled her to her feet at the same time he turned her away from the body. "First corpse?" he asked in such a casual way it made Mercy raise her eyebrows.

"No, first werewolf corpse though," she said in a quiet voice. "It's kind of horrible, isn't it?"

Andrei pursed his lips and nodded. "Yeah, it really is. We didn't have a choice."

"I know," Kit muttered. "I've never seen them change back before. Not like that." She looked at his arm and his bloodstained sleeve. "You did the same thing earlier."

"It's Mercy's cure. It gives me control."

Kit nodded, swallowing hard. She didn't look like she was going to pass out anymore, but she certainly didn't look well either. Whatever she was going through, she would need to deal with it quickly because they didn't have time to wait.

"We need to get out of this room," Mercy said as she pulled out her face wrappings and started putting her disguise back on.

Andrei glanced to her with a silent plea. Mercy shook her head.

Yes, Kit needed time. They all needed time. But there was no time to process and cope with what they were going through. Coping was the privilege of survivors. The gunshot had scared off some of them, but others would be drawn by the scent of blood. Mercy didn't have enough ammunition for all of them, and Andrei couldn't even scare one of them away with a claw to the face. These werewolves were determined.

Mercy went to Kit. "Do you have your wrappings?"

She nodded and pulled them out of her pockets. Her hands were shaking and felt cold to the touch, so she took them and started wrapping up Kit's face. "Don't freeze up on us. You do that and we're all dead."

Kit gave a short nod. She turned as though trying to look at the werewolf body again, but Mercy put a hand to her cheek and forced her gaze ahead.

"No," she whispered. "Curiosity is also dangerous. Trust me, I know."

"Okay," Kit whispered and didn't look again.

When they were done, Mercy turned to see Andrei had already put his disguise on. There were gaps in it from the missing bandages he had used on Mercy's wounds, but he still wouldn't be able to be identified. Good.

"Stay close," Andrei whispered before approaching the door.

Kit reached down and picked up one of the broken wooden chair legs. She pulled off a few pieces of wood before joining them at the door.

"I'm ready," she whispered, gripping the leg in one hand.

Mercy felt bad for all of them. None of them were prepared for this. She and Andrei had come to Crowsmirth to help people, not get caught in a blood bath between an enormous pack and a bunch of cocky hunters. Kit needed a solid place to call home, so she could recover from all the cruelty she endured. Instead, she was stuck in the crossfire with them, resorting to a chair leg as a weapon.

They only had to last until dawn. After that they could leave this place and never look back.

Mercy readied her gun as Andrei gripped the doorknob, mindful that she only had four bullets left and wishing she had brought spares from the mill. If they survived the night, she would never go on another task without extra ammunition. She would never be caught in a situation like this again.

As Andrei turned the knob, Mercy was close behind him, followed by Kit. Mercy had to hope that the rest of the inn had fared better than they had.

THE HALLWAY WAS DARK. The one other room on their floor had the door closed. It would seem peaceful if not for the sounds of werewolf howls and gunfire in the distance.

Andrei urged them all out of the room, then quietly pulled the door closed behind them. Mercy checked the stairwell, her gun aimed out in front of her. She saw nothing other than the rickety steps down to the fourth floor.

They were on the top floor which meant they had a long way to go to reach the ground level. They needed to find a room without windows where the roaming werewolves wouldn't be able to find them. None of them knew the layout of the inn or who else might even been staying there. For all they knew, the flimsy wooden doors were the only barrier they had between them and an onslaught. They had seen firsthand how easy it was for werewolves to reach the top floor of the five-story building. Every room was a potential threat.

She remembered the parlor downstairs where the leaders of the hunting party had planned their failed choke point. The parlor had heavy, wooden doors—unlike the flimsy ones used for the bedrooms—and most importantly, no windows that she could recall. That was why they had so many candles lit. That was a far more defensible location than their bedroom had been. Of course, that was also on the ground floor, the farthest point in the building.

There was also the question of the front door. She and the innkeeper had boarded it up, but with only three boards that was hardly much of a defense. She would have put up twenty if he had the supplies, but that was all he had. Clearly he hadn't boarded up a building before. Mercy had boarded up plenty of places in her time living with her father. She had seen werewolves tear through wooden boards like paper. It was foolish to expect that the front door wouldn't be a vulnerability.

She gestured for Andrei and Kit to follow and hoped she wasn't making a big mistake. That was a hope she had almost all the time these days. Together they crept down the stairwell—Mercy in front with her gun drawn, Kit in the middle with her chair leg, and Andrei bringing up the rear. Each step was taken slowly, being careful to make little sound. The wood creaked beneath them and every sound spiked Mercy's adrenaline.

Each floor had a wide landing, and at every landing they stopped and checked carefully. Shadows appeared like hulking beasts to Mercy's stressed mind, but she knew better than to be trigger happy. Four bullets, she reminded herself. Don't waste them.

Once she was certain the shadows were merely shadows, she glanced down the hall. Her heart beat so hard she worried every werewolf in the place could hear it. Down the hallway were four closed wooden doors. Mercy hoped the room behind each one was empty. She truly hoped they were alone in the building.

Down the next flight of stairs they went, slowly with barely a sound. Kit was no longer breathing fast like she had been upstairs, and Andrei no longer looked over his shoulder every second, making her nervous he would trip down the stairs in his panic. The next landing would be the third floor, the halfway point. Surely they couldn't have many people staying there. The innkeeper would have wanted them to be up above ground level as high as possible, right?

They stopped on the landing for the third floor. Down the hall, Mercy saw one door stood wide open, and her stomach dropped. A cold wind blasted from the room and she shivered. Likely another broken window, almost directly beneath theirs if she thought of the structure of the place. When they had scared off the werewolves from their room, had they merely moved on to another room? Had they indirectly caused more people to die?

She squinted her eyes and saw that the door knob was stained with blood.

Shit! Could a werewolf be wandering the hallways? Had the person survived? She strained her ears, listening for a click of a claw on the wooden floorboards or the heavy breaths of one of the werewolves. Distant gunfire only. Even the howls in the distance had stopped.

She locked eyes with Andrei. His mouth hung open and his eyes were wide. Mercy glanced to the room then back to him. Andrei nodded.

"Want me to change?" he mouthed, pointing at his chest.

Mercy winced. This wasn't an easy ask, and she knew it. If any hunter saw Andrei was partially transformed, he would be shot down the same as the others. She hated asking him, but they needed his strength and his speed. If werewolves were loose in the building, he wouldn't have time to change. They would be killed in seconds. She knew firsthand how fast and quietly a werewolf could be when stalking prey. She needed not only Andrei right now but his wolfish side, his animal side. Even if it hurt having to even ask.

They had no idea how many werewolves were in the building, in the stairwell, or even how many might try the various windows to get inside. If most of the hunters were dead outside, the inn would be the next target.

Andrei took a deep breath then extended his arm. Muscle grew, straining the sleeve of his shirt. Fur protruded from his skin, snapping seams and ripping parts of the cloth. He had only grown a single hand upstairs, but now he was transforming both arms. The unmistakable scent of brimstone hit her nose. Claws protruded from his fingers and his hand grew in size. The sleeve of his shirt ripped as more fur protruded. Blood dripped down his arm as the fur became more dense. Soon Andrei's arms didn't look like they belonged to him at all. They were large and cumbersome, but powerful.

Kit stared at him with open awe. To Mercy's surprise, she didn't speak once. Maybe she was getting used to dealing with the horrors they considered normal.

With a final shake, Andrei flicked off the remaining blood from his arm and lifted his black claws. He gave Kit a sheepish smile, clearly sad she had to see it. Kit took a deep breath and nodded. They all knew to be quiet. Silence was their only option to survive.

Once certain they were ready, Mercy led them down the next stairwell toward the second floor landing. They moved faster this time, and Andrei was slightly encumbered by his arms, but he managed it fine. Mercy held her gun out, despite her arms shaking. Her eyes continually swept through every hidden corner and crevice, searching for any movement or signs of a struggle.

Occasionally her gaze dropped to glints of blood on the stairs. She tried to avoid it, but at one point her boot slipped in some. She paused to catch her breath, making sure she didn't topple down the stairs. Kit's hand fell on her shoulder, reassuring her. Mercy swallowed down her own panic and continued.

There was no time to waste.

She thought the blood was from a werewolf at first

because of the different places where it was located, but slowly she realized it had to be from whoever had escaped the room upstairs. Transformed werewolves didn't need doorknobs. There was also no odor of sulfur on the blood, at least from what she could tell. The problem was, if Mercy could follow the trail so easily, so could a werewolf.

Second floor. Only one more to go. She stepped down onto the landing. Her stomach went tight when she spotted another door wide open. This time there was still an occupant in the doorway. The back end of a werewolf stood on all fours, its upper half hidden inside the room while its lower half remained in the hall. Its tail swished back and forth with delight.

Mercy was afraid to even breathe. She could hear it eating. It lapped at something with its tongue, chomped pieces of something in its mouth, and crunched down on what had to be bones. At its feet was a growing puddle of blood and an arm wrapped in green. She recognized the color. That green silk with the embroidery at the wrists must have been worth a fortune at some point. It was the man who had shot at her when she had gone to investigate the grocer's body that morning. Damn, had that really only happened that morning? He must have come to the inn to find safety, thinking the hunters would keep him safe. How wrong he had been.

Stars blinked in Mercy's vision and she forced herself to breathe. She couldn't help but imagine what it had to look like on the other side, and the thought made her truly want to run back upstairs again and hide behind the bed, even though she knew that was a terrible idea. Mercy was used to fighting her own instincts, but this was too much.

Kit moved closer behind her. Mercy felt her shaking against her back, felt her rapid, warm breaths on her neck. She couldn't flee, not when others needed her. If she was by herself, sure, why not, but not when she had Kit there depending on her. Not when she had Andrei at her side. She couldn't abandon Andrei to this.

The arm rolled to the side as the werewolf changed its angle. More bones crunched. It didn't matter. They would be dead if they didn't hurry. Mercy didn't have time to panic, to go into shock, or stare and wait for the inevitable slaughter. They needed to move.

She gestured to the others. Andrei nodded, but Kit continued to shake, staring at the arm in the doorway. Mercy grabbed her hand and pulled her out of her stupor, and then she gestured toward the stairs.

Kit gave a short nod. They darted for the stairs on the other end of the landing.

Mercy held her breath the entire time. Once they reached the stairs, she led them down toward the first floor. Almost to the parlor. Only a few more steps to go. Behind her, Mercy heard Kit padding across the floor, but she didn't hear Andrei's footfalls. She had to glance back to make sure he was with them. Sometimes he moved almost completely silently and she simply couldn't tell he was there.

He was there, but going down the steps backward, slowly. He kept one arm on the railing. Had the werewolf noticed them? Had it smelled them? She had hoped its fresh meal would keep it distracted, but then again, that hadn't been the case with Henry, had it? He had smelled her on the breeze even though she had almost passed him by.

Sweat trailed down Mercy's back as they finally made it to the first floor. What she saw there made her suck in a breath.

AT THE BASE of the stairs, Mercy stood holding up her gun and she shook her head at the impossible sight before her. The front door was gone. Not just broken, but completely gone. Pieces of the boards they had used to board it up littered the floor. The door sat in two pieces across the room, splintered in half like plywood instead of a solid slab of thick pine. Near the front counter they had used maybe an hour ago, a blood trail caught her attention. It continued behind the desk. Mercy was glad she couldn't see where it led, but it also meant she couldn't see what was hiding behind the counter either.

A growl from behind it sent a chill down her spine. She turned to see the werewolf from the second floor landing standing now at the top of the stairs. Its eyes glowed red in the darkness. When it bared its fangs, she could see its entire muzzle was covered in blood.

"Run!" Andrei said in a half-animal, half-human cry. Blood soaked through his pants as his legs grew longer. Hair sprouted out of his cheeks and his face elongated. He was transforming into his full werewolf form.

Mercy knew it had been an option the entire time

they were in Crowsmirth. She knew she might need his strength and his ability to match the werewolves blow for blow, but she never wanted it to come to this. Any hunter might shoot him and she still wasn't sure if he had full silver immunity. She certainly didn't want to test it here.

Turning away as tears burned in her eyes, Mercy raced across the lobby, past the open doorway and the front counter. Another werewolf head popped up over the edge of the counter as she darted across the open space, some gory entrails in its mouth. Had that been Oscar, the innkeeper? It didn't matter. Whoever it was, they were dead.

Kit whimpered behind her, forcing Mercy to keep moving despite her instinct to freeze at the horrific sight. They both ran into the parlor, the same enclosed space the leaders of the werewolf hunters had used.

Mercy glanced quickly around the room. Only a few small windows in the back and plain wooden walls. That was good. A few candles remained lit from the meeting earlier, illuminating the space. It looked empty.

Hearing snarls from behind, Mercy turned to close the door behind them and saw the werewolf behind the counter clawing and lumbering over, its amber eyes turning red. Fully in his werewolf form, Andrei awkwardly rushed down the steps, his clothes hanging in rags on his body. His teeth and claws were stained crimson.

Mercy held the door a crack, looking between the werewolf coming over the counter and Andrei. His golden eyes met hers. Mercy felt her heart skip a beat.

"What are you doing?" Kit pleaded, her voice hoarse and wavering. "Close it! If either gets in here, we're dead!"

With a grimace, Mercy held up a hand, wordlessly urging her to stop talking. Kit did, but her terror had already been heard by the werewolf that had scrambled over the counter. Andrei sprinted across the lobby, stretching his body out to its full length. The werewolf on the counter gave a deep growl and curled inward before lunging for the parlor door.

Kit frantically stepped away from the door with her hands covering her mouth.

Watching carefully, Mercy urged Andrei on silently. *Come on, Andrei. Don't make me trap you out there to die!*

Andrei leaped halfway across the parlor at the same time the werewolf did. Just as Mercy was about to pull the door shut, Andrei slammed into the werewolf in mid-air. He clawed at the other werewolf's face with a speed and frenzy Mercy had never seen before. The werewolf fell hard against the wall, and Andrei landed once before leaping inside the meeting room, and skidding across the floor. His claws had trouble getting purchase on the wooden floorboards. As the werewolf outside shook himself off, Mercy closed the door. She bolted the lock fast and turned to see Kit about to run to the back of the parlor.

"It's okay," Mercy whispered. "It's just Andrei."

"Andrei?" Kit asked in a soft voice.

Andrei had hit the opposite wall pretty hard. but he was getting up, regaining his footing and shaking his head. Mercy went to him and wrapped her arms around his neck. His muzzle, chest, and arms were covered with werewolf blood and he smelled terrible, but she was so grateful to have him.

"Are you okay? Are you hurt?" she murmured into his ear.

Clearly distressed, he tried to pull away from her.

"Hey, it's okay. Come back to me." She placed her hands on either side of his muzzle and rubbed his cheeks. Shaking from head to tail, his amber eyes glanced over to the door instead of looking at her.

"Andrei," she whispered, keeping her voice as calm as she could.

He whimpered.

"I know, you're still ready for the fight, aren't you? Still riding that adrenaline high. You're okay, I think we're safe in here."

She rubbed the tufts of fur on his cheeks and stroked the bridge of his nose, ruffling the scruff on the top of his head and massaging an ear. Finally he stopped shaking and turned to look at her. His amber eyes glinted with preternatural light in the darkness.

It reminded her of the night he had transformed before the entrance to the laboratory. At the time she thought she would die, but he didn't attack her. That night, without a drop of Liquid Lead in his veins or even her partial cure, he came and laid beside her, calm and content for a time. It was almost like this. He had that same fiercely protective look in his eyes. When he had heard Leyda and Thomas in the distance, he had that same defensive posture too. Strange as it was, she honestly found it endearing.

"Trust me. I think you scared that werewolf off for good. He's going to have trouble seeing after tonight," Mercy smiled. "You're done fighting. You can change back. It's safe." She rubbed at his shoulder blade, holding his gaze steadily. Finally, she noticed his posture relaxing.

Andrei closed his eyes and took a deep breath. Slowly his body reverted back. The muzzle shortened back into his face. His claws retracted into the human hands she knew and loved. His fur pulled back into his skin, making a sound like walking through coarse grass. He almost looked human. Then his spine cracked, and he fell to the ground, whimpering from the pain.

"Shh," she whispered, rubbing at his shoulder still, feeling the mixture of sweat and blood against the heat of his body. His spine cracked and reformed again and again. Mercy counted one time. It happened twenty times during each transformation, give or take. It wasn't consistent like she had expected it to be. She waited until the final one seemed to be finished. Andrei lay on the ground, sucking in deep breaths and trembling.

"You were brave to do that back there," Mercy whispered. "I know that wasn't easy."

He swallowed before pushing himself up into a seated position. "I didn't know what else to do," he grunted through his partially human mouth. His jaw cracked a few times before becoming fully human again.

"Shh, don't talk yet. I know it has to hurt to talk."

He gave a short nod. She stroked his neck as his hair grew again, short, coarse, and cropped like he liked it. His sweat glinted in the thick coils. She dragged her fingers through them with a smile. She had watched the process countless times, back before he had been given her cure. It was nice to be this close to him for once, nice to be able to help him through it and ease him back into her arms again.

When he was back to being fully human, back to being the Andrei she loved, she wrapped her arms around him and hugged him tight. He gave a short laugh and put an arm around her.

"I can't believe you kept the door open," he whispered.

"I wasn't going to lock you out there with them. You would have died. I would have kept that door open all night if it meant keeping you alive."

He was silent a moment. "Next time, don't wait on me. Close it. I can handle myself, you can't."

"Andrei…"

"No, I mean it." He pulled away from her despite her best attempts and met her gaze. As close as they were, their foreheads were almost touching. "Next time, close the damn door and leave me out there. You two could get eaten or worse, bitten! I can hold my own. You can't."

He was right, of course. If she only had herself to worry about, it was an easy choice, but then there was Kit to consider. The poor girl hadn't ever been given the chance to live. Mercy had no right risking her life.

It wasn't fair when Andrei did this. All she could see were his gorgeous lips moving, and she wanted so badly to kiss him. She was doing a pretty good job of holding her own considering he was completely naked in front of her too. It ruined her.

She huffed in frustration. "You know I can't concentrate when you're like this."

He blinked in confusion. "Like this?"

"Yes, when you're naked."

Andrei's eyes went wide, and a flush came to his cheeks as he looked down to confirm he was indeed naked. He pursed his lips as he looked up to her again and Mercy smiled.

"Um, here you go," Kit muttered. "I pulled it off the table. I don't think anybody cares if you wear it."

Mercy and Andrei both glanced over to her. Kit had her back to them, but she held out a tablecloth behind her toward them. She kept her gaze carefully aimed at the opposite wall. "*Please* don't start making out when I'm right here. It's really gross."

Mercy shook her head with a laugh. "I'm sorry, Kit."

Andrei took the tablecloth and wrapped it quickly around his waist.

"Yeah, sorry. I forgot about… you know, clothes."

She flapped a hand at him. "It's fine. Fine. Just don't mention it. Like at all."

He shrugged, and Mercy's gaze lingered on his shoulders and arms far longer than necessary. "Sorry, Kit. It's a side effect of the transformation. It can't really be helped."

Kit nodded and swung her arms at her sides. "Good to know. Next time I'll bring you a spare set of clothes, so you're not this embarrassing."

Andrei gave a nervous smile. "Thanks, I think."

Kit shook her head. "Are you dressed yet?"

"As dressed as I'm going to be."

She gave a nervous glance before noticeably relaxing. "Oh good. That was really awkward for a minute there."

Mercy got to her feet. "I'm sorry, Kit, I never meant to get you involved with all of this. I thought we would be back at Farrell Mill with you by now where it's safe. Not putting you in even more danger."

Kit gripped her elbows and glanced to the bolted door. It took her a moment to respond. "Just because I'm scared doesn't mean I don't want to help. I've felt trapped by werewolves for months, but I never really saw them as people until now." She glanced over to Andrei with sympathy in her eyes. He couldn't meet her gaze. "They're not beasts out there. They're people. They can't help being what they are any more than I could help being trapped at that house."

Mercy put a hand on her shoulder. "I know how painful that can be. I felt the same way once too. It's difficult."

Kit gave a short nod and pursed her lips. "I know it sounds crazy, but I feel like I owe them. They got me out of that place. They killed my captors." Tears came to her eyes and her voice broke. "I know I can help, Mercy, I just don't know how."

Her words tore a hole in Mercy's heart. She knew what it was like to feel helpless yet pulled toward something bigger. She had felt the same way in Farrell Mill when she was cleaning out werewolf cages and dealing with Carter's insults. It was terrifying at the time, but she had known she could be more if merely given the chance.

She asked, "How old are you, Kit?"

"Eleven, why?"

Mercy smiled. "You're stronger than I was when I was your age," she admitted. "Don't worry, I think you'll find where you need to be."

Tears spilled down Kit's cheeks and soaked her bandages. She wiped at her eyes in frustration. "I don't know how you can see me crying like this and say that."

Mercy squeezed her shoulder. "Because I've been where you are."

Kit stared at her with a mixture of disbelief and confusion.

"Don't ever be ashamed of tears. It means you're moving on, that's all."

Kit pursed her lips and gave a short nod. She was clearly trying to hold back tears that still threatened to fall. Mercy went to let go, but Kit pulled her into a hug.

"Thank you for rescuing me," she muttered before pulling away again and wiping at her eyes.

"No problem." Mercy wished she could explain how much Kit reminded her of her younger self. Instead, she turned to find Andrei standing by the door, his ear pressed up to the wood. Her smile dropped, and she quietly went to his side.

"What do you hear?" she whispered.

"Nothing," he said. "It's almost too quiet out there. Mostly I hear the occasional gunshot in the distance, but that's it. I was worried that one was going to attack again, but I guess I kicked their butt enough to make them run away." He grinned at her. "They realized they didn't stand a chance."

Mercy elbowed him which only made Andrei muffle a laugh.

"We should still make sure this room is secure. If we can guarantee that, maybe we can get some sleep tonight."

Kit gave a bitter laugh, having regained her composure. "For you, maybe. I'm not sleeping at all tonight."

10

———————

THE PARLOR

THE PARLOR WAS a large room with a wooden table that took up most of the space. Wooden chairs sat askew around the table, either from the meeting earlier or from Kit removing the tablecloth from the table. Two lit candles sat on side tables near the front of the room, giving plenty of light where they stood, but leaving the rest of the room dark. Farther in the back, Mercy made out a few armchairs, but the back of the room was impossible to see.

She and Kit had glanced in earlier when they first came inside, but they hadn't had time to make a thorough check. Mercy wasn't as concerned about werewolves hiding in the shadows as she was about werewolf hunters. They could be just as dangerous as werewolves, and she didn't like the thought of someone watching Andrei's transformation from the shadows. Mercy pulled out her gun. Andrei came up beside her.

"You don't think there are werewolves back there, do you?" he asked, confusion lacing his words.

"No, but there could be hunters."

His eyes went wide and his lips parted. He had originally looked like he wanted to go with her, but he pulled back.

"Can you smell anyone?"

He shook his head. "All I smell is the blood of those werewolves outside and you two. In my defense, there is a lot of death tonight."

She huffed. "That's an understatement. It's a slaughter out there."

He lowered his voice, moving closer to her. "I'm also afraid I'll lose myself again if I throw myself into sniffing anything out. Like in the woods."

Mercy met his gaze. She remembered him following the trail of werewolves. It was how they had found Kit's home. She also recalled him turning around with dilated eyes and taking a minute to recognize her. It had been frightening. He almost hadn't changed back a few minutes ago too. She had to calm him down before he could. It was probably best if they limited how often he had to fully transform.

She put a hand on his arm. "I used to be a hunter, remember? Let me handle this."

He bit his lip. "If I had my disguise, I would be better. But like this, I feel… exposed."

"Don't feel bad about that. You know what they're capable of. You saw those traps outside."

He dropped his head and nodded. "Yeah, I saw them."

She motioned for the door. "Keep an eye on the

door. That should be our only exit. If they come inside, we're trapped."

He leaned closer, his lips inches from hers. "Please be careful."

"I will," she promised.

He kissed her. His lips were warm and soft against hers, and Mercy forgot herself for a second. He went for the door while Mercy burned with want. Finally she sighed. He was a terrible influence on her, but she wouldn't have it any other way.

Pulling her mind away from Andrei, she made her way toward the back of the room. Two armchairs sat near the back of the room near a stone fireplace. Both were unoccupied. Cushions had once been on the chairs, but they clearly had been worn down years ago. Mercy examined the fireplace next. It was made of stone so it was probably pretty solid. However, it was larger than she liked and she hoped the chimney flue was closed. A large werewolf might not fit, but a smaller one might. She crouched down to the floor and leaned forward to see if she could look up the chimney. That's when movement caught her eye.

She froze and glanced up to beside the stone mantel of the fireplace. A small window had been inset there, maybe a foot tall and a couple of feet wide. Her stomach dropped. The room wasn't as secure as she thought. Another window framed the other side of the mantel. A smaller werewolf could easily fit through. She thought back to Kit's house and realized she couldn't rule it out as a weak spot for the wall too. Especially if they could see or smell them through it.

Mercy backed away from the fireplace, noting a door at her side. Made of cheaper material than the main door to the room, it was closed, so she still didn't know what was on the other side. Damn. Too many unknowns. She didn't like that at all.

Keeping her gun at the ready, she reached out with her left hand and opened the door. It took her a moment to realize what she was looking at.

It was a large walk-in closet. Shelves lined the three walls filled with fabric, stacks of plates, crates, and cleaning supplies. Mercy checked the corners, but it was clear nobody was hiding in here. At least that ruled out one immediate threat.

She holstered her gun and pulled down some fabric before stepping back out with supplies in her arms.

"What is all that?" Kit asked, looking curiously at her. She stood with Andrei still at the front of the room.

"More tablecloths to match the one you took off the table," she said.

"Perfect, maybe I'll get a whole outfit," Andrei grinned.

"Keep your voice down," she hissed and Andrei shrank back.

"Sorry!" he whispered.

Mercy held up the thicker woolen cloth. "Kit, can you help me out?"

She hurried over and followed as Mercy led her to the windows. "Think we can get these up like curtains?"

Kit eyed the windows nervously. "Yeah, let me see if we have any nails we can use."

"No hammers," Mercy said. "We can't draw attention to where we are."

She frowned, "Right. Hopefully they'll hold."

Working in silence Mercy and Kit put the first curtain up. Kit had found a few nails in the storage closet, but without the use of a hammer, it was harder to get them to keep the heavy fabric up. Mercy held a corner in place, looking for any movement through the edge of the window while Kit worked.

The windows looked out onto an alleyway beside the inn but Mercy didn't see much activity. She kept trying to figure out what she had seen from the corner of her eye earlier that had made her decide to cover the windows, but she kept second guessing herself. It could have been the shoulder of a werewolf, but it could have also been a gun held on someone's shoulder. Either way, it shouldn't be so still outside, not with the sound of howls in the distance. She ought to have heard rounds of shooting. The stillness from the hunters was unsettling.

"Okay, got it," Kit cried.

Mercy glared at her and it took Kit a moment to realize she hadn't whispered. Her eyes went wide, and she slowly put a hand to her mouth. Neither of them moved. Mercy stared through the small gap beside the curtain, barely breathing and looking for anything that might indicate danger. After several minutes of nothing, she let out a heavy sigh. She was about to give the all clear, but then a looming shadow stepped down the alleyway.

All the muscles in her body went rigid. She tried to

keep her arms from shaking as her stomach dropped. A large brown werewolf came into view, its eyes amber as it tilted its head, listening intently. Mercy watched it step into the moonlight, illuminating the blood on its jaws, arms, and chest. It occasionally licked at its mouth like a cat before sitting back on its haunches and cocking its head to the side again.

It was so patient. She had never studied them without Liquid Lead before and it was unsettling. Why wasn't it moving on to join the rest of the pack or return to its kill? The longer it sat, the more unnerved she felt. From everything her father had taught her and all the observations she had made at the mill, this was not how a werewolf was supposed to behave.

She thought of a statue, a frozen lake, a boulder… anything to help her remain perfectly still. The werewolf stretched again, giving a big yawn, and then it walked down the alleyway toward them. Mercy dared not back away. The movement might get its attention. It moved to the back of the alley and raised its nose into the air to sniff. Mercy was shaking, trying not to show it, trying not to let the fabric in her hands move and betray their location. Finally the werewolf returned to the entrance of the alley and departed.

Mercy refused to drop her guard. She refused to drop her arms either.

She wasn't sure how long she held that position, five minutes, maybe ten, but by the time she allowed Kit to put up the second corner and let her arms drop to her sides, they throbbed with pain.

Kit didn't say a word. She didn't need to. Mercy saw

how shaky her hands were as she worked. They worked in complete silence, communicating through gestures instead of words. Neither of them wanted a close call like that again.

Once the first curtain was secure, they moved on to the second one. Mercy kept a lookout while Kit worked. Mercy saw no more movement outside.

They were lucky. That was a rare gift, especially in a place like Crowsmirth. She didn't expect it to happen again.

It also meant that there were so many dead bodies that the werewolves weren't having to hunt for more food. They had eaten well. Never a good sign.

———

"I'M sorry I was so loud," Kit said once they were all sitting on the floor together near the front of the room. "I could have gotten us all killed."

"You made a mistake, that's all," Andrei said. He had pulled out some of the spare tablecloths and wrapped them around his shoulders. The embroidered white flowers on the red fabric actually looked cute on him.

"We got lucky," Mercy said. "These werewolves are killing anything that moves tonight. As long as we stay away and don't draw attention to ourselves, we should be relatively safe from them in here. If we were the only people in this city, that door and those curtains wouldn't keep them out."

"Yeah, we would all need werewolf cages then," Kit said with a nervous laugh.

Andrei shook his head. "We only have to last longer than the other people, is that what you're saying?"

Mercy sighed. "I'm saying that when we're dealing with this many, yes. Either that or actually have a decent plan of attack. Even the Tortoise couldn't have stood up to so many. I honestly don't know how you dealt with it, Kit."

She looked down at her hands and started twisting them together. "I don't think I ever had this many of them at my house. I think the hunters drew them to town tonight. They wanted as many as they could get, and I guess they got their wish." She shook her head and rubbed at her eyes.

Andrei stretched and yawned. "If you think it's safe to get some shuteye, Mercy, then I'm all for it. I'm honestly exhausted. I don't know how I dealt with transforming like that every night."

Mercy reached over and took his hand. "I'm glad you made it back to us."

"Me too," he admitted, smiling.

Kit looked between the two of them, clearly uncomfortable again. "I wasn't joking when I said I didn't plan on sleeping. Ever since Ma and Pa died, I don't sleep at night. Werewolves aren't exactly the best at a sleepover, you know?" She gave a nervous laugh. "Don't worry, I won't doze off. I'll pace around the room a million times first."

"Are you sure?" Mercy asked. "We could take shifts. You're going to feel it tomorrow."

"Then I'll sleep on the drive to Kanta," she said with steel in her voice. "I am too anxious to sleep tonight. We've had too many scares already and I don't need another. If you two want to sleep, go for it. I won't sleep until dawn."

"Only if you're sure," Mercy said. She didn't fully support it, but it was clear Kit wouldn't budge. It made her nervous for any of them being asleep. The werewolves weren't the only enemies they might run into, but she was worn out. She was hungry and thirsty too, but surely they all were. It didn't do any good to mention that. All they could do was wait it out until dawn and hope to escape Crowsmirth safely.

Mercy got to her feet and stifled a yawn.

"Where should we sleep for the night?" Andrei asked.

The armchairs not only looked uncomfortable, but they were too close to those windows. Sleeping underneath the dining room table just felt weird. So that left the walk-in closet.

"What about the closet?" she suggested.

"It would be helpful in case we get any non-werewolf surprises in the night," Andrei said. "I don't have a disguise anymore and to be honest I'm not too keen on having my face seen. We're not that far from Kanta, and I used to come down here to make deliveries almost every day. I don't know who might know me around here, you know? Not that any of those people are probably alive now."

Mercy nodded. "I saw some white bed linens we

could tear up for you in the morning," she yawned again.

He grinned. "Definitely in the morning. You're going to fall asleep standing up at this rate."

Kit gathered the thin cushions from the armchairs and put them on the floor in the closet for them. She was trying so hard to make up for her mistake earlier. Mercy felt bad because it really hadn't been her fault. Kit hadn't been raised to be a werewolf hunter like Mercy, and she hadn't lived in the harsh conditions of a werewolf camp like Andrei. She was still learning.

After Kit had arranged the cushions to sort of look like a mattress on the floor, Mercy said, "Thanks, Kit. I'm sorry if I've been hard on you. I don't mean to be. It's just… it's been a long night."

She gave a genuine smile. "I know. I think we'll all sleep easier once we're out of Crowsmirth."

Andrei laid down on the cushions and gave a sigh of relief. "I feel better already. Come on, Mercy, you can pretend it's a bed if you close your eyes."

Mercy followed him inside with a grin, removing the bandages from her face. "You're so weird."

"You two lovebirds sleep tight," Kit said with a smirk before closing the closet door behind them.

Mercy couldn't suppress a chuckle. This was hardly a romantic situation with werewolves eating people in the streets, let alone a safe place for anything like that. Still, she couldn't help watching Andrei roll out the red embroidered tablecloth from around his shoulders to use as a blanket.

He looked too good without a shirt on. That didn't help.

———

"YOU GOING to stare all day or are you going to come join me?" Andrei patted the spot on the floor beside him, a smile on his lips as his lidded gaze making her squirm.

Mercy flushed. She didn't know what to say or even what to do. "You really are ridiculous sometimes."

"I know." He grinned.

Mercy put her gun aside along with the satchel of injection needles she had intended to use on the werewolves in the camp. It pained her to look at them. They had such high hopes when they had left Farrell Mill that morning. New helmets, a new vehicle, and they had just finished up with the camp in Kanta. She really had thought they were getting the hang of this. Now everything had turned out so differently.

Curling up, she took a few minutes to even out the thin cushions that were the only way to soften the feeling of the hard floor. Finally she curled up against shirtless Andrei. Breathing deeply, he stared up at the shelves of supplies over their heads. His chest rose and fell, the embroidered white flowers on the red tablecloth moving with him. Remnants of blood still lingered his skin from his transformation earlier. He had clearly exerted himself, but she didn't care. She wrapped her hands around his arm, breathed in the scent of him, and pulled him close. He snuggled closer, but his mind was clearly a million miles away.

"What are you thinking about?" she asked as she snuggled him beneath the tablecloth.

"You're going to think I'm ridiculous."

"It's too late for that."

He laughed. "Fair."

"So what is it?" she asked.

He bit his lip. "When I used to be an apprentice at the apothecary in Kanta, sometimes my work lasted overnight."

He pulled his arm free of her grip and draped it above her head and over her shoulders. It made a warm fuzziness form in her belly as she curled in closer to his bare chest. She leaned her head on his bicep and stared into his face. In that moment, she loved him so much it hurt.

"I would experiment with finding the latest chemical marvel or the newest medicine powder, trying to find something we might sell. Often I could only do the work at night when the laboratory was free, and they didn't need me on the main floor. I'd bring a couple of blankets and curl up on the floor overnight, staring up at shelves of chemicals above my head. I know it sounds weird, but it was very relaxing."

"You're right, it does sound weird." She snickered. "But I bet you would have made an amazing apothecary yourself. I've seen how well you know your chemicals and compounds. If you hadn't trained me, I would have never figured out how to make the cure."

He turned away and licked his lips. "I mean, I'm not

as skilled at it as you are. For me, it was fun to experiment with and maybe get a bit of praise, but you dove into it completely. I could never do what you did. You took the basics from me and took off with it, Mercy. You have a knack for it. I wish I could latch onto things like you do. You learned in months what it took me years to learn."

Mercy leaned up, pulled his chin toward her, and kissed him. Short and far too chaste, it said what she couldn't find the words for. He blinked at her in confusion when she ended the kiss and nestled back down beside him.

"Stop it," she said. "It isn't a competition. We collaborated. I wouldn't have done any of that without your support. You helped me translate Thomas's chemical work. When I first started out, it looked like a foreign language to me. Besides, it doesn't even matter now. I won't listen to you pull yourself down after you literally just saved our lives back there."

He gave an awkward smile. "I mean, you have a gun. You could have protected yourselves without me back there. You didn't really need—"

She pushed down the tablecloth and propped herself up on her arms, cutting him off with another kiss—longer this time. She savored his taste, his earthy scent, and the heat of his soft lips against hers. It sated that burning need in her, at least for a moment. When she finally pulled away, he leaned forward.

Mercy didn't cuddle up to him yet. She hovered over him so he couldn't look away from her again, and so he couldn't avoid her words or her gaze. "Yes, I could have shot them, but they would be dead. We're here to help werewolves, not kill them, remember? I already killed one upstairs, and that was one too many for me."

He glanced down to her mouth before meeting her gaze again. A smile tugged at the corner of his mouth. "If I say no, will you kiss me again?"

"No!" She laughed, and he laughed with her. He wrapped his arms around her and pulled her down on top of his chest. Her heart fluttered with his touch, with his warmth. She felt safe in his arms. They kissed again. His arms wrapped around her waist and she put a hand into his hair. Finally they pulled away, breathing hard and staring into each other's eyes.

"You're a beautiful person, inside and out," she said.

"And you're my jerk." He didn't miss a beat and Mercy couldn't help but grin. He laughed, and it reverberated through his body. She loved it.

She dragged a hand through his thick hair. It had gotten longer since he had been at the camp, but she liked it. His eyes closed, and she smiled down at him. He was falling asleep, and she wished he wouldn't. She wanted to kiss him again, wanted to feel his lips against hers, but she knew not to do it while he was asleep. That wasn't right.

She put a hand up and traced his lips before putting the finger to her own lips at the memory of his kisses.

"I love you," she whispered.

"I love you too," he muttered in a half asleep haze.

Mercy grinned and slid off his chest to nestle up against him again, wrapping an arm around his stomach. Somehow they were perfect for each other despite coming from completely opposite worlds.

She wasn't sure how she had gotten so lucky to have him in her life after all they had been through. In that moment, she knew she would do anything for him and it was amazing to have someone to love who truly loved her back, even when he was half asleep.

Despite the terrible trauma that had led them here, she would always be grateful for him. She would always thank whatever fates had flung them together, even if it landed them in a storage closet in a place like Crowsmirth.

Mercy hugged him before closing her eyes and giving in to sleep.

11

SECRETS

THREE LIGHT RAPS on the door jerked Mercy awake.

For several confused moments with her mind bleary from sleep, she thought she was at home again and had slept in. Her angry father would scold her for being late with her chores. Years of training had made her jump when her father made any request. The panic that filled her told her if she didn't move fast, she would pay for it later.

She turned to look at the door, an apology on her lips, but before she could speak, reality slammed into her brain. This wasn't her modest bedroom. Instead of half-completed sewing work and materials for creating darts for Liquid Lead, she stared at crates of cleaning supplies, a damaged push-broom, piles of tablecloths, and a slew of dust bunnies. She blinked in confusion, trying to make sense of where she was. This wasn't her home. This wasn't even her bedroom. Right. She was in Crowsmirth at the inn after surviving one of the longest nights of her life.

She let out a shaky breath. That wasn't her father at the door. He had died years ago.

The reality settled her nervous stomach and the panic that flooded her body. She had grown so familiar with that feeling as a child, as an adult it was strange to feel it consume her again. Slowly the feeling slipped away and Mercy breathed easier.

Three light raps came again, followed by Kit's whisper. "Mercy? Andrei? Are you awake?" She groaned. "I *really* don't want to come inside. Please don't make me."

Mercy cleared her throat. "Yeah, I'm awake."

"Oh, thank goodness! I didn't want to see you two… well, you know." Kit cleared her throat and Mercy grinned. "Anyway, it's dawn. I thought we should get out of here while we can."

"Thank you for keeping watch. We'll be out in a moment."

"No problem!" Her footsteps padded away from the door.

Kit had a good head on her shoulders. Mercy doubted she would have been able to stay awake all night listening to the werewolf howls in the dark by herself. Especially after such a crazy night. They were lucky they found her. They were also lucky she joined them.

That was two strokes of luck, Mercy realized with a frown. Too much good luck led to bad luck. That's what her father had said at least. Or was it the other way around? She pulled herself from her musings and focused on her lovely sleeping companion.

Andrei was still fast asleep. When she fell asleep she

had been curled up against his chest beneath his arm. During the night, they must have turned away from each other so that their backs were touching. She sat up to see he was curled inward with his knees up against his chest.

Damn, he was beautiful. Shirtless, his brown skin gleamed in the morning light that peeked beneath the closet door. The tablecloth had fallen to his hips and Mercy knew all too well what he looked like below. His face was relaxed, which made her smile. She couldn't remember a time when he looked so peaceful. She wished she saw it on him more often.

It felt like an untouchable moment, something that should be revered. She tried to take it all in, his body beneath the embroidered tablecloth amid the dust bunnies and cleaning supplies. The light across his skin and the peace on his face. Oddly enough he looked more beautiful against the dingy closet. He was absolutely perfect, and she had to wake him.

He hadn't moved an inch while Mercy talked to Kit through the door. Apparently a full transformation wore him out just as much as it had before he got the partial cure. She felt terrible destroying the moment, but they needed to get moving. That didn't mean she couldn't have fun waking him.

She got onto her knees, and then lowered herself across him, certain he would wake up any moment. But his eyes didn't flicker.

"Andrei," she whispered, resting her hands on his shoulder and laying her cheek on his chest.

He mumbled something incoherent in his sleep.

"Andrei, it's time to wake up."

Slowly his eyes opened and his initial confusion melted away to amusement.

"I could get used to wake up calls like this." He motioned to turn over toward her and she lifted up so he could. Then he wrapped his arms around her waist and pulled her close to him. She leaned down to kiss him and he met her halfway. It was brief, but it was enough.

"Do we have to get up?" he whined.

"Yes, we do. Kit's waiting on us and it's already dawn. We've got to get out of Crowsmirth without being discovered by the hunters. If those leaders come around here again, I don't want us here."

He frowned but didn't say more. Mercy pushed up to her feet and opened the door, squinting a little at the morning light.

"A little help?" Andrei asked.

Mercy turned back toward him with a smile and helped him to his feet. She winced as she heard his joints crack. He was always stiff and sore after a transformation, apparently the partial cure didn't prevent that.

"Are you doing okay today?" she asked.

"More or less." He stretched and she heard more joints pop. "Remember the werewolf that climbed over the countertop in the lobby? There was a body back there, I could smell it. I don't know if the innkeeper made it."

Mercy shook her head. She had come to the same conclusion too, but the whole conversation she had with the man seemed odd. "He said his name was Oscar. He didn't seem to like the hunters, but I couldn't figure out why. Maybe if I had more time, I could have learned more about him."

"They probably just didn't pay for the room or something. Maybe they took over the place. Don't be so quick to assume he would have helped us if he knew what we were here for." Andrei yawned.

Mercy sighed. He was right, of course. As much as she wanted people to be on her side, she had to be cautious. Though if she had been too cautious, she might never have gained Andrei as her boyfriend or helped Kit escape her home. Sometimes trusting people was worth the risk. "I guess it doesn't matter," she said. "He's dead now."

"If he's dead, maybe we can use his clothes," Kit said. At the front of the parlor, she was lacing up her worn boots. Mercy glared at her, but Kit merely shrugged. "I know, it sounds morbid, but he's dead. He can't use clothes anymore. And Andrei needs proper clothes and a way to hide his face. Looking like that, they're going to think he's a werewolf who escaped the gunfire last night."

She was right. Mercy needed to stop ogling Andrei and get her head back in the situation. This wasn't the time to let her hormones overwhelm her logic. They weren't out of Crowsmirth yet. If they weren't careful, they could still end up dead.

The wrappings she used were thankfully still in her pocket, so she began applying them as she spoke. She mentally had to thank Leyda for making her wear the wrappings so often. She hardly had to think while putting them on now. "I'll go out and see what I can find. Kit, stay here in case you need to cover for Andrei. Get your disguise on so nobody can see your face. And Andrei?"

He blinked at her with worry, clearly aware his presence put them all in danger. Her heart broke for him.

"Don't worry, we'll get this figured out." Mercy gestured behind him. "For now, go hide in the closet."

Andrei grimaced but headed back inside. He glanced back to her. "Be careful."

"I will," she said.

Kit trailed behind her when she went to the door, trying to put on her disguise but failing.

Mercy fixed the last of her wrappings and then helped Kit with hers. She was clearly frustrated.

"I'm not very good at this," she muttered.

"It took me a while to get these right too, don't worry." Mercy helped with her bandages, making sure they were properly secured in the back. "Speak in a low voice if you have to speak at all."

"But, Mercy, I can't pass as easily as you can. What if they find out I'm not a guy?"

Mercy put a hand on her shoulder. "Do your best. Remember, if you pretend like you know what you're doing and that they're the ones in the wrong, you're more likely to fool them. Most people won't question you."

She nodded, but the fear was clear in her eyes. "I think if anybody shows up, I'll just channel my inner Mercy. Does that work?"

Mercy chuckled. "Sure, that's fine. Whatever works, to be honest. Listen. I'll knock four times in a row, pause then knock two more times to let you know it's me."

She nodded, touching the knots tied on the back of her head. "Be careful out there. I'll lock up behind you."

"Thanks," Mercy whispered. She took a deep breath and headed out into the inn, bracing for anything.

SUNLIGHT POURED in through the missing front door of the inn. Bloody werewolf tracks mixed with the dirt and leaves that had blown in from outside. If Mercy concentrated, she could probably make out the path the werewolves took coming indoors, sniffing the air, and then moving upstairs. She thought of the bloody door knob and the arm of the man with the green housecoat.

She shuddered.

Daylight took away many of the unknowns. It revealed corners, exposed corridors, and revealed what she had suspected all along. Blood was also spattered on the walls and the door to the parlor. She wondered if that was from the werewolf Andrei mauled as he ran for the room. It was hard to tell from all the remnants of blood in the room.

Mercy turned toward the front counter. Large claw marks tore down the front of the wooden counter, but it was hard to tell why. Had they smelled someone hiding back there and tried to climb on top? Or were they from the werewolf who emerged last night and jumped at Andrei? She thought of Oscar the innkeeper and swallowed down the lump in her throat. Thick blood pooled out around the base of the counter, seeping out from whatever was behind the counter and drying in the morning light.

She stared at the blood, hoping it didn't belong to Oscar, but Andrei assumed it did. Also the odds of anybody else being down here last night was slim. Andrei also needed clothes. He was depending on her to help him escape this damn town. She needed to find anything that would make him look more like a victim and less like a werewolf, but she didn't have Kit's courage. She had admitted to stealing from corpses before, but could Mercy do the same?

Bracing herself, she stepped around the back of the counter, careful to avoid stepping in the blood. Behind it lay a body that no longer had a face or a throat. The chest and belly were ripped open and already flies swarmed it.

Mercy didn't think about who the person was. She couldn't allow herself to do that. Instead, she looked at the claw and bite marks. One leg had been dragged off to the side, the thighs chewed on so bad that bone was visible.

Mercy swallowed down the dryness in her throat.

It was too much carnage for a single werewolf to have done alone. The thought made the hair go up on the back of her neck. Werewolves working together to take down prey. Never in her worst nightmares had she expected that to be possible. She thought back to the fence at Kit's home and the flipped truck last night. Maybe the enormous pack was different.

She thought back to Kit's home. They had worked

so hard to kill a single girl in a cage that they toppled the second floor. The entire group was in such a frenzy that they had been tearing through the wall and wooden beams to get to the door of her cage. Werewolves weren't that good on their own. These were too smart. Too organized. She pursed her lips. Even the werewolf hunters last night hadn't succeeded at taking them down, as organized and prepared as they had been. Was it simply the sheer numbers of the pack, or was it something else?

Mercy shook herself and squatted down by the body to do a closer inspection. Her limbs vibrated as her heart pounded in her chest. It was one thing to experiment on werewolves in a controlled laboratory setting, but it was very different seeing one of their victims up close. She wanted the science part of her brain to take over, to analyze it objectively instead of the knee-jerk repulsion she felt building inside. Her instincts screamed that she should run away. She had worked so hard to overcome the weak stomach Leyda had more than once berated her for having. Truth be told, she really thought she had overcome it, but now she knew otherwise.

Running away wasn't an option. Hiding in the parlor wasn't an option either. They had to get out of here. She put a hand out to the wall to steady herself. Squeezing her eyes shut then opening them again, she focused on the clothes. The person had been wearing leathers and hides: a hunter. Possibly one of the young ones still working as an apprentice. She saw no gun. Maybe it had been wrenched away outside and then the two werewolves carried the body in here to feed, away from the rest of the pack.

If situations were only a little different, that could have been her. If she had been born a boy and hadn't been sequestered away by her father, she could have easily met the same fate.

Mercy started breathing harder.

Clothes, she reminded herself. That's what she was here for. She needed a disguise so they could leave and get back to the Tortoise. This mission had gone wrong in so many ways, it would take a week before they could even try to return to Crowsmirth again. They needed to get back to the mill, reconvene with Thomas, and plan their next steps. That meant she needed to do more than stare at this corpse all day.

She slid a foot forward to climb to her feet, but a weight fell on her shoulder as she stood. She gasped and spun around.

Oscar stood behind her, blood splattered all over half his face. He had a rifle propped up on one shoulder. He wore the same clothes from the night before, only now they were almost unrecognizable from the amount of blood staining them.

"You survived." He gave a chuckle, looking her up and down. "I'm glad to see it."

"I thought you died," she sputtered, a little too high-pitched, but Oscar didn't seem to notice.

He glanced up to the ceiling. "I heard the glass shatter upstairs and worried you all got eaten in the night." He had a weird tinge to his smirk she didn't like. The hand resting on her shoulder didn't make her feel any better either. It was supposed to be comforting, but it felt more like a warning.

"We survived, but it wasn't easy," she replied, dropping her voice as low as she could to avoid suspicion. She pushed his hand off her shoulder—it felt like dead weight—and took a step back from him. One foot settled with a squish in the blood. She winced.

"Survival never is easy, is it?" He studied her face, frowning a little. Mercy realized she was in a corner with the mangled body on one side and Oscar on the other. She hadn't expected anyone to be alive in the building, but if they could survive the night so could others.

"Mercy… that's your name, isn't it?"

Her body went taut, but she kept her face neutral behind the bandages, not wanting to let anything slip. She opened her mouth to protest.

"Actually, sir, it's Mark."

He waved a hand and shook his head, a glint in his eye. "There's no need to pretend with me. I knew your father well. Surely he told you about his old friend Oscar?"

Mercy just stared at him, too shocked to know what to say.

"I was there on the day you were born. Aw, it's a shame Solomon never mentioned me. He grew distant in later years. I heard about his passing. He was a good man."

Goosebumps broke out on her arms and her mouth went dry. The hair stood on the back of her neck. Did she try to keep the ruse going when he had already seen through it? Or should she come clean with the truth?

Part of her wanted to know more. How did this man know her father? The more she thought about the many unanswered questions, the more she wanted to know.

Oscar took her gloved hand and gave it a squeeze. "I know he kept you locked away most of the time. It must be upsetting to hear strangers talk about him, but he was a good friend of mine." He shook his head. "I'm sorry you have to disguise yourself in this manner, but I certainly understand the need for it."

"No, I—" She sighed. "I mean, we don't have a choice. You know what trafficking is like around here."

He frowned. "Oh, I know. I had a daughter taken once. Never saw her again." His expression grew dark, but then he brightened again almost as quickly. "But don't you worry. Your secret is safe with me. I won't tell a soul."

Mercy felt the knot of panic in her chest loosen just a little. "Thank you. It's been stressful, between the barricade and the werewolf attack last night."

He stepped back and Mercy was grateful to get out of the corner with the corpse. "So tell me, how can I help? You mentioned the barricade, so I assume you have a vehicle nearby?"

She nodded. "Yeah, we do, but I need to get a spare change of clothes for the tall guy who was with us last night. He… had a rough night."

He scratched at the scruff on his chin. "I may have some spares in the back. Want to come help me look?"

Her mental warning bells went off so fast she blurted out, "No." She gave a sheepish grin. "No, thank you. I think I'd prefer to wait here if that's alright by you."

"Certainly." He went for the stairs with his limp but stopped and turned toward her again. "And if you see any of those horrid hunters snooping around, tell them I have it all well in hand."

The statement made her uncomfortable, but she couldn't say why. "Sure, I can do that."

He nodded and climbed the stairs slowly, heedless of the bodies slumped across it in the corners and on the landings. Everything about Oscar made her uncomfortable, but that was probably because he had seen through her disguise. She wondered if he had known who she was last night and if so, why he hadn't said anything when they boarded up the door together.

Through the front door opening, she saw groups of hunters moving around the town, several of them dragging bodies. During the day it was hard to tell what bodies belonged to a werewolf and what belonged to a human. Upstairs in the grocery store across the dirt path, shadows moved. They were trying to throw broken furniture or something out of the window. Oddly, it took three of them to push it out.

When the morning light hit it, she realized it wasn't a torn up chair or bedding, but a horribly mangled body covered in so much blood that she couldn't tell the head apart from the groin.

The trio shoved it out the window, but Mercy closed her eyes and turned away before she heard the thump of it hitting the ground. The sound made her feel light-headed, and she put a hand against the wall.

Turning around, she put her back to the carnage outside. A hand to her lips, she smelled the blood and sulfur permeating her clothes and the morning air. It was her weak stomach again, just as Leyda warned. She had thought that through her experiments and her nightly observations of Andrei's transformations, she had beaten it out of her, but clearly she still had a long way to go before she would be made of steel like Leyda. She still couldn't watch the grotesque cleanup outside and she wondered if she would ever overcome it.

"Are you alright?"

Mercy looked up to see Oscar standing at the base of the stairs only a short distance away. She hadn't heard him coming, and this wasn't exactly a silent building. There went her alarm bells again. Honestly, this was his inn, of course he could move around it easily. She needed to settle down.

"I'm good. It's just a lot to take in, I guess." No matter how she tried to word it, she still felt inadequate. She pulled away from the wall so she wouldn't lean on it like a crutch.

"I think I found a pair that should fit him. If it doesn't, let me know and I can dig up another pair." He gave her a clean pile of white linen. "And here are a few cloth rags for…" he gestured to her face. "For all of that he'll need."

Mercy nodded her appreciation. "Thank you. I know he'll be grateful for this." She turned back toward their room and she felt Oscar's hand on her shoulder, heavy and firm.

"Oh, and if you don't mind, please don't tell them

about me. I mean, about us talking. I would rather them not know about me and your father. The more people who know, the harder it is to keep a secret, after all." He gave a forced chuckle. Or maybe it was a genuine chuckle, and she was being ridiculous again. Still, she couldn't deny the chill that went down her spine at his hand on her shoulder again.

"Why not?" she asked, unable to contain her curiosity.

He hesitated for just a moment. "Your father didn't have the best reputation with werewolves or hunters, and I would rather not be associated with him, if you get my meaning."

Mercy nodded. She too had found her father's reputation made things difficult. It made sense that Oscar would want to distance himself, especially since he was running an inn.

"I won't tell anyone if you keep my identity a secret too," she said glancing to his hand. He gave a slow nod and removed his hand from her shoulder.

Good. Hopefully he got the hint. Mercy went back to the room and gave her synchronized rap for Kit. It was quiet inside. That meant they had taken her advice. Mercy glanced behind her once more and saw that Oscar had vanished.

For a man with such a bad limp, he moved like a ghost.

12

AN OLD FRIEND

"THEY FIT ALMOST PERFECT!" Andrei cried, unable to keep the relief out of his voice. "How did you even find these? There's not any blood on them." He pulled on another boot, which was a little big for him, not that he complained. Mercy guessed that living in the woods as a werewolf made him flexible with clothing sizes.

"I got lucky looking through dresser drawers upstairs," she lied, keeping her eyes averted. She hated keeping secrets from them, but there was no way they would approve of her and Oscar's truce. It was a risk to trust anybody, even when they helped.

"Why do they have to be so white though?" Kit asked with a sigh. "He looks like he's going to work as a chef or something. No way we can convince anybody he's a hunter and should be traveling with us."

Mercy frowned. Kit had a good point. They were trying to blend so they could escape Crowsmirth and Andrei was painfully out of place right now, even with a new set of clothes.

She picked up the pile of bandages Kit had made from the scraps and twisted them between her hands. Andrei got to his feet and strolled over.

"So, what's your plan?"

Mercy grinned. "It's funny you think I have a plan."

"Don't give me that. I know that look! That's your planning look." He glanced to Kit. "I've seen it a lot. I can practically hear the gears in her head working."

Mercy chuckled. He wasn't wrong of course, but it made her happy to hear him call her out. It was all part of their elaborate flirting game, which would eventually need to go somewhere other than sleeping in a closet together. A fluttery feeling came to her chest at the thought, but she pushed it back down. Not now, hormones. Damn. She glanced down to the fabric strips in her hands. "You won't like it."

He shook his head. "I never like it, but I'm also ready to get out of here. So do your worst."

She laughed as she turned to him. "Remember, you gave me permission."

She separated out a handful of the strips and gave them to Kit. "Head out to the lobby and look around the front counter. You'll see a bunch of blood there. Soak up as much as you can in these and bring them back."

Kit's eyes went wide as she took the fabric strips. "Really…?"

"Yes, really. And be quick, there are a bunch of hunters roaming the streets out there."

"Do I need to lock the door and do the special knock to get back in?"

Mercy shook her head. "Not this time. Just be quick, okay?"

A questioning look banked in her eyes, Kit glanced over to meet Andrei's gaze, but then she headed out to the lobby. Mercy wasn't sure what Oscar's interest was in all of this, but she had a feeling Kit wouldn't run into any trouble running out and back in again. She didn't trust herself to go out there again without the group because she wanted to unravel Oscar and find out what he knew about her father. She didn't trust herself without them beside her. Sometimes her curiosity could be a real pain in the butt.

"I guess you didn't see any trouble out there?" Andrei asked, fishing for information. She wasn't going to give him any.

"It's clear. How do you think I went up and searched through the dressers without a problem?"

He nodded, buying her lie. Damn, she was too good at this.

"So… the blood."

She sighed. "I told you it wouldn't be fun. When we put the blood on, keep your mouth closed. I don't want any getting digested. You would probably be fine being, you know, what you are, but I want to play it safe."

"Okay," he said, a little defeated.

"Now hold still while I start the wrappings."

He gave a short nod and held still. Mercy began the base wrappings. "I'm going to cover up one of your eyes to make this more believable and to distract from the rest of the look. You threw yourself into a fight last night and saved us, but took on some grievous injuries. It's not a full lie, right?"

"Having lost an eye once, I can definitely lend some believability to it."

Mercy wrapped over one eye, careful not to hurt him or completely obscure his vision. Kit came back with the bloody wrappings, wrapped in what looked like the dead man's shirt to keep them from dripping everywhere. It was embarrassing how much less squeamish Kit was than Mercy. The mere thought of taking the dead hunter's shirt off as gruesome as he looked made her feel lightheaded all over again.

Instead of leaning against anything again like a crutch, Mercy gritted her teeth and focused on her work. She took the bloody scraps and squeezed blood out all over the front of Andrei's white shirt and pants. She even took the dead man's shirt and rubbed more blood over Andrei's chest and torso. Finally she wrapped the bloodiest pieces over his "missing" eye. By the time she was done with the look, Andrei looked like he could barely walk, which was perfect.

Mercy took a step back to admire her work. Clearly she had been focused. She had worked up a sweat and was panting a little. "There we go. I think even Leyda would be proud of this."

"I sure hope it fools them," Andrei said, his voice muffled behind the thick fabric strips that weren't as giving as the cheap, worn fabrics they had access to at the mill.

"It better," Kit said, rubbing the blood off her hands and onto a clean spot on Andrei's shirt. "'Cause that was pretty disgusting, even for someone who regularly steals from corpses."

Mercy blinked at her. Kit had spoken so casually it made her skin crawl. It was one thing to suspect it, but very different to know that she did that regularly. No wonder she had a stronger stomach than Mercy. She had to, in order to survive.

"Can we get moving before I smell this too long? I'm actually getting hungry and that is kind of freaking me out right now," Andrei shifted uncomfortably.

"Seriously?" Kit gaped. "You're hungry wearing that?"

"He's a werewolf, remember?" Mercy reminded her. "Just because he transforms different doesn't mean he's fully human either."

Kit gave a short, shocked nod. "Yeah… I guess. Let's get out of here before Andrei licks at the bandages."

"I won't do that," he said, frustration seeping into his voice. "I'm not that hungry."

Mercy put a shaky hand to her head to quell the throbbing headache coming on. Maybe she needed food, maybe that was her problem. She didn't recall them eating anything since the dry foods in the Tortoise last night. That was what, over eight hours ago? Or more like twelve hours ago? Damn.

Andrei went to the door with Kit as they stepped out together. Andrei put his arm over Kit's shoulder and she helped him pretend to hobble out into the lobby and through the front door.

"I'm coming," Mercy called but her voice was small. It was as if she couldn't get enough air in her lungs to be heard. She pushed her legs to move as the pulsing headache grew worse.

What was this? Had she exerted herself too much with Andrei's disguise? Was this a migraine brought on by stress and lack of food or water? Whatever it was, it was bad.

***

MERCY STUMBLED her way out of the room and into the lobby. The pool of blood near the front desk made her stomach do a flip-flop. She took a deep breath to steady herself then turned and walked out the front door. The sun was high over the treeline now and the world was far too bright. She blinked, unable to keep her eyes open against the painful light. Even lifting her hand to shield her eyes didn't help much. She blinked in desperation at the sea of light around her, forcing her legs to move forward, one step, two, three.

She tried to call out for Andrei and Kit, but her voice was little more than a whisper. It felt like every time she opened her eyes to brave the sunlight, they were a little farther away, a little more out of reach. Neither of them looked back at her. Not once.

Mercy's legs no longer obeyed her. They refused to move, so she stood, teetering in place, unable to get a full breath of air into her lungs. The headache throbbed so badly she felt like her head might explode. When her ears began ringing, Mercy knew she wouldn't be able to catch up with her friends.

She fell to her knees, but it was muffled like it was

happening to someone else. She felt the impact rattle her, but she couldn't bring herself to care. A puff of dirt drifted into the air from the impact, wavering to her face, determined to take away what little clean air she could breathe.

Her torso fell sideways, her head hit the ground and turned the world on its side. She breathed in the dust, watching as Andrei and Kit made it past the barricade of vehicles. At least they made it. At least they got out. Thomas had her notes to make more of the cure if they needed it, and Andrei would help him. They would get by without her.

Oh Andrei… The memory of his warmth came back to her from their shared kiss that morning. It had been far too brief. Tears came to her eyes. Her death would destroy him. She couldn't let that happen. She had to fight this, whatever it was. Succumbing was not an option.

She needed to get up, push herself to go on. Her friends were just ahead, just a few small steps ahead, and she needed to go after them. She rolled over onto her stomach and the world tilted again. The throbbing of her skull came back with a vengeance. She reached a hand out and dug her fingers into the dirt, determined to claw her way to them if she had to.

"There, there, child. There's no need for all that." Oscar appeared from the side and nudged her hand aside with his foot like she was little more than a doll. His boots crunched in the dirt by her head as he crouched down. They looked like hunter boots, not the thin soles of an innkeeper's shoes. Fingers gripped her chin and turned her face so that the sun bore down on her. She whimpered, closed her eyes tight and tried to look away, but his hold on her was strong.

He chuckled and whispered. "My goodness, how much of that powder did you breathe in? You've really done a number on yourself."

Finally he released her chin and her head dropped down to the dirt again. Mercy breathed in the dust as her foggy brain tried to make sense of it all. Powder. Was that why he put his hand on her shoulder again and again? She even turned to his hand that last time, probably breathing in even more of it. She wanted to scream at him, to fight him. Anything. But her body wouldn't obey her.

Oscar helped her to her feet and slung one of her arms over his shoulder. Instead of helping her walk, he mostly dragged her. But to others he probably looked like he was helping an injured hunter. Damn him. The tips of her toes made grooves in the dust on the ground.

They didn't return to the inn. Somehow that was worse. At least she knew what was inside the inn and could plan an escape, but that didn't seem to be Oscar's plan. Instead, they went around the building and came across another barricade in the back. It was mostly abandoned now. The hunters were probably counting heads of werewolves, gathering the dead, and calculating profits. This wasn't considered a dangerous place anymore.

Dappled sunlight filtered down from the trees, making it harder for Mercy to keep her eyes open. She smelled the forest and felt the branches catch on her clothes. Oscar was panting as he dragged her, his limp becoming more pronounced. She wanted to ask questions, to figure out who this man was and what he was going to do with her.

Oscar shifted her to the side and opened the door of a vehicle. Mercy's heart leaped into her throat. She opened her eyes and glimpsed a truck with a flatbed in the back. A groan from the back alerted her that they weren't alone. Had he captured someone else too? He picked her up and laid her down on a seat, strapping her in with the seat belt. He was taking her somewhere, somewhere far away, to some place nobody would be able to find. They had talked about human traffickers at the inn. He even mentioned his daughter had been taken. She never imagined he would be one.

Mercy broke out in a sweat, but she couldn't lift a limb to do anything.

He shut the truck door closed, and she tilted to the side, leaning against the door. She smelled the old, worn leather mixed with sulfur. A werewolf had bled here. She thought to the person in the back. Were they a werewolf? Or some other woman who had been hiding in Crowsmirth?

Oscar crawled in on the driver's seat. The vehicle took a minute to catch. Each time it whined, Mercy hoped the Tortoise would crash through the trees. She wanted Andrei with her so bad she could cry. Finally, the old truck turned over, and she felt the vehicle lurch as they drove through the woods and then hit the dirt road.

Mercy shut her eyes tight against it all. Hot tears slid from her eyes onto the sulfur-smelling leather.

"I still can't believe you thought I was a friend of your old Solomon Pinkerton." He chuckled. "He raised you, child. You ought to know that the man had no friends."

Mercy's heart sank at his words. As a drug-induced slumber pulled her toward unconsciousness, her father's words came back to her as a promise and a rage.

Survive for me.

To be continued in:
The Fury of Kanta

AFTERWORD

Werewolf attacks, mass hunter barricades, and a romance that's starting to heat up. Here we are at the end of Book 3 of The Wolves of Kanta series. I never imagined this is where Mercy's story would go when I first wrote The She-Wolf of Kanta years ago, but I love it!

Hunters was tough tale to grasp. I knew I wanted to take Mercy and Andrei beyond the borders of Kanta to see what the rest of the world looked like outside of Farrell Mill. It turns out it's not faring very well. Crowsmirth came as a name for the town long before the strange crows who live there. And while I had a vague concept of Kit's character, I didn't know who she was going to be or how she had survived on her own for so long until I discovered it. Pen hitting paper truly creates magic.

I hate to leave a book on a cliff-hanger, but sometimes that's just how the story works out. Mercy had been a little too lucky for a little too often and it was bound to catch up to her. Oscar is quite messed up too, so it won't be good for her.

Thank you for sticking with me on this twisted adventure. If you enjoyed Mercy, Andrei, and Kit, and the horrifying world they live in, I hope you'll consider leaving a review on your favorite storefront and maybe recommending this series to a friend or two. I'm an independent author so all the support and love my books can get the better.

I'll see you again for Book 4: The Fury of Kanta. Rest assured, there will be fury.

Thank you again, dear reader!

Marlena
August 1, 2022

Weird western, werewolves, vampires, short story

Night Feeders

Mystery, film noir, humor, short story

The Mysterious Disappearance of Charlene Kerringer

 **Join the Mailing List** 

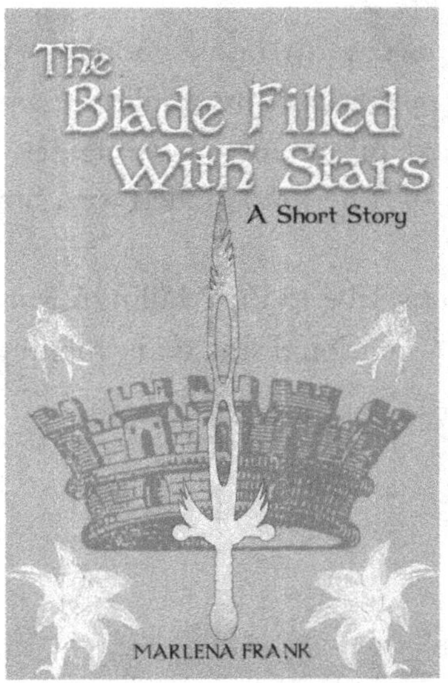

The Blade Filled with Stars

A kingdom is under siege from a familiar enemy. Families and friends are pitted against each other without reason. Slaughter is imminent while the winged Queen Khafil soars overhead. Desperate and terrified, Anna works with her sister, Lilah, to summon aid from their mother's ancient spell book.

Determined to save their people, the sisters

summon Death to help them, but Death is not easily swayed. Neither of the sisters are prepared for the consequences.

Want a peek behind the scenes?
Want to preview my books before they get released?

Get exclusive access to book goodies, giveaways, and cover reveals by joining my mailing list. Not only will you get notified of all my new releases, you'll get an exclusive copy of The Blade Filled with Stars.

Subscribe to the Mailing List at:
http://marlenafrank.com/mailinglist/

ACKNOWLEDGMENTS

The Hunters of Kanta was a fun but difficult book to write, and like every book, authors need plenty of support to trudge through toward publication. I have a bunch of people I want to thank for helping me create this book and encouraging me with this series.

Lara Zielinksy, my fantastic editor, who has been with me for both Blood of Kanta and Hunters of Kanta. She has been incredibly punctual, helpful, and insightful with her edits. I honestly don't think this book or this series would be nearly as powerful without her. Thank you for all your help!

A big thank you to my older sister, Kelley, who encouraged me to stay on track with my timeline even as we dealt with the plague and other setbacks. There were times I considered pushing things back because it felt like there was a deluge of obstacles against us, but she believed in me and in my work. I'm so grateful for her help during these tough times.

To my parents for always giving wonderful feedback and being endlessly supportive of me as a creator. They have often been my bedrock when I've run into crashing waves. They keep me grounded and help me get on my feet when things get rough. To my aunt Charmaine for being there for every win no matter how small. She is truly an endless cheerleader and I am so grateful to her.

Thank you to Candace Robinson for being a sounding board and for giving me some wonderful ideas on marketing. We're always brainstorming how to weather this independent author work, and she is always there to help when I run into trouble or have questions. She is truly a wonderful friend and an amazing author.

To Carla Lewis, an incredible author and talented friend, thank you for your support and your feedback. She is always there for me and I never forget that. I appreciate all of her help and guidance with this book and practically every piece I write. She is amazing.

One of my long-standing readers who happens to be an incredible friend as well, Donna has been a Ko-Fi supporter of mine from the beginning. She was a reader of my work years ago when I was just starting out as an indie published author and is always one of the first people to read and review my books. Most recently she helped me get through a tough place with my small press I used to publish through. I am so incredibly grateful to her.

Finally, thank you dear reader for being here. I hope you have enjoyed this book and that you'll consider reading more. These books wouldn't be here without you and I never forget that. Thank you for supporting me!

ABOUT THE AUTHOR

Marlena Frank is the author of young adult fantasy and horror novels, short stories, novellas, and book series. Many of her books have hit the bestseller charts, including her debut novel, Stolen. Her work has been praised by Readers' Favorite and featured in De Mode of Literature Magazine. Her stories have appeared in anthologies such as Emporium of Superstition, Catstruck!, Heroic Fantasy Quarterly, Georgia Gothic, and The Sirens Call ezine.

Although born in Tennessee, Marlena has spent most of her life in Georgia. She lives with her sister and two spoiled adopted cats. She serves as the Vice President of the Atlanta Chapter of the Horror Writers Association, is an active member of the Science Fiction and Fantasy Writers Association, and is an avid member of the Atlanta cosplay community.

She is also an INFJ, a tea drinker, and a wildlife enthusiast.

Support her on Ko-Fi: ko-fi.com/MarlenaFrank
Follow her at: MarlenaFrank.com